A NOVEL
PITBULLS
IN A SKIRT

MIKAL MALONE

PUBLISHER'S NOTE:
This book is a work of fiction.
Names, characters, businesses, organizations, places, events and incidents are the product of the author's imagination or are used fictionally.
Any resemblance of actual persons, living or dead, events, or locales is
entirely coincidental.

Library of Congress Control Number: 2007940747
ISBN: 0-9794931-2-9
ISBN 13: 978-0-9794931-2-6

Cover Design: Davida Baldwin www.oddballdsgn.com
Editor: Hightower Editorial Services
Graphics: Davida Baldwin
Typesetting: Hightower Editorial Services
www.thecartelpublications.com

First Edition

Printed in the United States of America
10 9 8 7 6 5 4 3 2 1

What's Up Babies,

Wow, I'm not gonna lie, the publishing game is a lot of fuckin' work! The funny part about it is, I self published my first novel "Rainbow Heart" way before I got with Triple Crown and wrote, "A Hustler's Son" and "Black & Ugly". But for some reason, I don't remember so many steps being involved. Roll with me through my journey right quick.

First I hire one of the hottest graphic artists in the game for my covers. And I must tell you, Davida Baldwin is a graphic artist genius! The moment I saw the covers for our first titles, "Shyt List" and "Pitbulls In A Skirt", I like to have lost my mind! They were exactly what I was looking for and we couldn't wait to make the announcement that, *The Cartel Publications* was ready to GO!!!! Wrong!!!!

After weeks of our covers floating around the net, a gentle angel pointed out that one of our covers had a terrible error. I had the word "Thrown" instead of "Throne" on the front of such amazing artwork. How embarrassing and I must add this was all my fault! I must have thanked Virgo a thousand times because she saved me a lot of heartache by letting me know *before* print. Sure many people saw the oversight, but only one person took the time to let me know. Others told me casually while talking about something totally unrelated. "*Toy, what's up girl? And by the way, your cover is fucked up.*" Funny right? I know but it's true I swear it! These same people were individuals I considered friends. Anyway, I took the casual exclusion of information as a welcome to the cold, cold world of urban literature. And those same people can kiss my ass and watch my dust as I scratch, crawl and pull my way to the top!

Everybody not being out for you is just one of the lessons I've learned by diving into the publishing game. And you know what? After all the drama, I'm still here and could honestly say that there's no place I'd rather be. I smile in the face of adversity and push myself even harder now.

Pushing myself even harder brings me to my next order of

business. Like Charisse Washington, Vice President of my company mentioned in her letter in our first title Shyt List, with each book we drop, we'll pay homage to an author who has opened doors. With that said, I'd like to show some love to,

"Nikki Turner"

Nikki murdered them with her first hit "A Hustler's Wife" and continues to blaze trails. Thanks for keepin' it hot Nikki! We love what you do.

Also special recognitions goes out to the ladies who help spread the word around about our titles.

"The Cartel Publications Pep Squad"

Jessica aka "Lyric" (Squad Captain), Ms. Toya Daniels, Erica Taylor, Shawntress, Kim Gamble, Victoria "Tori" Johnson, Crystal, Lisa aka JSQueen625, Kariymah, Kendell and Chauntice.

So…sit back and chill, and enjoy Pitbulls In A Skirt. It's one of my personal favorites and I know you'll love it too. These ladies look good on the *"Throne"*. **smile**

Until I hug you later….

T. Styles
President & CEO, The Cartel Publications
www.thecartelpublications.com

DEDICATION

This is dedicated to the brothers behind the wall. It's easy for people to forget about you if you're hidden from view. Let's rise up, make a positive impact, and be seen for the men we are and not who we use to be.

Acknowledgments

I'd like to thank my better half, and the best part of me. You've never left my side, even when I wasn't there for you. Boo-boo, I know I did you proud on this one.

To Mom Dukes, thanks for giving birth to me. Don't worry, we gonna get our relationship where it needs to be, one visit at a time.

To my seed, stay in school and keep it together. You see where bein' a knucklehead gets ya, don't walk in my shoes. Walk around them.

To all the authors who books get me through my time. Thanks. You inspired me more than you realize. Stay up, and keep puttin' out them hits.

PITBULLS IN A SKIRT

If you make it through the gates that house *"Emerald City"*, one of Southeast D.C.'s deadliest housing projects, you'll run into four females with colorful ski coats and designer jeans. And if you don't belong, you'll quickly find out what they have hidden in the Marc Jacob or Louis Vuitton purses they hold closely to them, because these females aren't just pretty faces. They are the women taken out of their beds and placed on the throne by the hustlers they loved.

This is their story…

CHAPTER 1

THE HUSTLER'S BALL
DECEMBER, FRIDAY, 10:30 P.M.

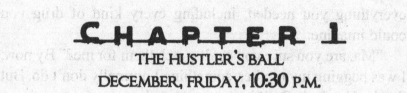

It had been an hour since I hung up with my mother and I was still pissed.

I couldn't believe she waited until the last minute to tell me she couldn't watch her own grandkids! Tonight was the wrong night for her to pull this bullshit on me. Mr. Melvin's yearly Christmas party, which we call the Hustler's Ball, was in an hour and it was obvious I wasn't gonna make it.

Mr. Melvin, the property manager, started the parties at the community center in Emerald City to try to stop the violence. However, what he didn't realize was all he did was breed every hustler in D.C. that was in the game. It was the only time we allowed the security guards to open the gates for outsiders, but not without checking the list we provided for them first. We owned Emerald City and everybody in it. Nobody made a move without clearing it with us first. Even though D.C. government paid the guards, they received their *real* orders and *real* money from us.

With five buildings and twelve floors in every one of them, Emerald City was one of the largest projects in the city. Originally named the Frederick Douglas Housing Projects, the project acquired the nickname Emerald City because all the buildings had emerald green awnings.

1

PITBULLS IN A SKRT

Tucked behind the gates of Emerald City was a barbershop, a beauty salon, Murry's food store and an arcade, everything you needed, including every kind of drug you could imagine.

"Ma, are you sure you can't watch them for me?" By now, I was begging my mother, something I normally don't do. But for the Hustler's Ball, it was warranted.

"I'm positive. Bye, Mercedes!" *Click!*

She hung up on me! I cannot believe she hung up on me! Man! I can't stand her sometimes!

I opened my bedroom door and walked into the living room. I started contemplating whether I should ask my son, who was sitting on the couch playing a video game, to watch his sisters for me. Asking Cameron Jr. was almost as bad as asking my mother. He had his own mind now and that was somewhat scary. He was growing up so fast and I knew it was just a matter of time before he wanted in the game and in the life he'd been raised around.

Big Cameron already had him counting the cash we collected from the runners at the end of the week. And as long as he learned about the ropes from his father, I had no problem with him dealing when he was ready, but he had to be *ready*. I loved this life and everything about it. Between the power, the money, and the look on my man's face when he came through the gates and saw shit was still intact, this life excited me. There is no other feeling that can compare, outside of the way Cameron makes me feel when we made love.

"L'il C, you sure you don't wanna make $200 tonight?" I asked him while he was playing Madden 2008 on our 50-inch plasma screen TV. "It'll help your momma out a lot."

I sat down and put my arm around him. He looked irritated and I could tell he knew I was trying to butter him up.

"Doin' what, Ma?" he asked, never taking his eyes off the

game.

"Watchin' your sisters," I responded, playing with his hair.

He looked at me with his big eyes and that beautiful curly hair like I had just asked him to do the worse thing in the world. Letting me know he wasn't going for it.

Cameron, Jr. was 13 years old and helped me out a lot with 8-year-old Chante and 4-year-old Baby Crystal but lately Chante was becoming too much for anyone to handle. And I made a promise not to force him to watch his sisters unless I was handling business, and I always kept my promises.

"Come on, Ma! All Chante gonna do is get on my nerves when you leave! She makes me sick sometimes! She cries the moment you go plus she don't listen."

"Calm down boy. I ain't gonna *make* you do anything. But you know the Ball's tonight, and your Aunt Stacia and Dex gonna be here in a minute to pick me up."

Truthfully, I could've paid anybody to watch them, but I like them to be around their own things and in their own place. Plus I didn't trust just *anybody* in my apartment. And most of the muthafuckas I knew, who would have jumped at the opportunity to earn $200 for 4 hours, were fucking with that shit. So sending my kids with them or letting them watch them at my place was out of the question.

Between all of our clothes and our expensive furniture from overseas, I had over $200,000 worth of shit in my apartment. We did real well with the money the drug life gave us, so I didn't need anybody taking it from me because I messed around and let someone in my apartment that could later plot to rob us.

"If I say no you gonna be mad?" he asked.

"How can I be mad at you?" I rebutted. Looking into my son eyes, it never ceased to amaze me how much he looked like his father. "I'm just gonna be upset that's all." I continued hoping he'd change his mind.

"Well...I don't wanna do it," he said continuing to play his game and avoiding my stare.

"Alright then," I said walking slowly to my room. My tired attempt to give him time to change his mind. "Let me go tell your aunt's the bad news."

I walked to my closet, which held Cameron's and my clothes. It was so packed that I could hardly find anything when I wanted it. Looking at the packed closet, I let out a frustrated sigh. I would be so happy when Cameron became a lieutenant, so we could finally move out of Emerald City. The bottom line was this, no matter how much money we had, we were still living in the projects. I knew it even if people around me chose to forget.

I grabbed my white Eddie Bauer ski jacket and zipped it up all the way to the top. I was just about to leave my room, until I remembered to grab my Marc Jacobs bag with "My Bitch" tucked inside it. My Bitch was the name I gave to the 9 milli'. I never left my house without it. I hadn't had to use her yet, but I was willing to if need be.

I walked toward the elevators and as always the stench that met my nose reminded me of how nasty my neighbors were. I could immediately smell the dirty apartments and trash which sat behind their doors for far too long.

While waiting on the elevator, Derrick, one of the grimiest niggas on my squad walked up to me. Derrick was a hard worker, but he had a tendency to try me from time to time, so I was constantly putting him in his place. At first, I used to tell Cameron when he got me wrong but Cam started getting mad, saying that they'd never respect me if I kept running to him over everything they did. So I started handling stuff on my own, and I only came to him about the big shit.

"What up, Mercedes!" he asked as we both waited on the

elevator.

"Nothin'." I did my best to keep my tone even, reminding him that we weren't friends.

"You goin' to the ball tonight?" he asked, still trying to spark up convo.

We stepped into the elevator and I met his stare with one of my own.

"Look." I paused, "You know I'm not with the small talk and shit. So unless we talkin' 'bout business, we ain't talkin'."

"Yeah...uh...I know," he said as we walked off the elevators looking all salty and shit. "I'm just tryin' to be cool with the female I report to, that's all."

I didn't respond. I let him walk ahead of me because I hated people walking behind me, especially somebody as grimy as Derrick. When we approached the exit to the building, I saw my girls on the steps. *Shit! They gonna be blown like shit wit' me.*

Before he walked outside, I remembered I didn't find out the status of the dope fiend who gave him $50.00 in counterfeit cash in exchange for some of the purest heroin in Southeast.

"Derrick!" I yelled before he pushed open the building's door. The cold air hit my face quickly before the door slammed shut again.

He turned around and walked over to me. "Yeah."

"What happened with that head? You handle it?"

"Yeah," he smiled as he smoothed the side of his face with his right hand and grabbed his chin. "We handled that shit. I think his funeral was last week."

"A'ight but next time get back with me."

"Yeah...Okay," he paused, clearly still upset that he had to take orders from me instead of Cameron even though it had been over three years now. "I'll try to remember that."

"You *WILL* remember."

He nodded his head and turned toward the door. When he walked through it, the night air hit me hard. It wasn't a match for my Eddie Bauer jacket, but it was hell on my jean-clad legs. You'd think by now I'd be used to the cold air since I had to man my post for twelve hours a day for the past three years.

The first thing I saw when I opened the door were tight ass cars driving through the gates. *Damn! Rashawn from NY really did get the Lamborghini! She's a lucky muthafucka!*

There were all types of high-end cars navigating the streets. Mercedes, which happens to be my favorite, BMWs, Range Rovers, Bentleys and Acuras flooded Emerald City's gates headed to the ball. Some playa's had went all out, showing up in chauffeured Navigator and Hummer limousines. Seeing the cars got me horny and now I was even madder at my mother. For a second I even contemplated *making* L'il C watch his sisters. But like I said, I never break my promise.

I saw my girls handling business as usual in designer dresses and fur coats while waiting for Stacia and Dex to scoop us up. The community center was a ten minute walk because EC was so big, so we were better off driving which only took about two minutes.

I laughed when I saw them dressed up while handing out orders in front of the building. And as always, Yvette was the loudest.

"*Look*...don't tell me you got it if you don't, Dramon! If shit ain't right when we get back, you might as well leave town. I'm not fuckin' around wit you!"

"I got it, Yvette," he said with his hands in his pockets while shaking his head with confidence. "Ya'll ain't got shit to be worried about tonight. Me and my soldiers holdin' shit down."

Most of our soldiers were between the ages of 16 and 21. Cameron said Dex liked them that way because they showed respect and above all else, they were hungry for that money. He said the older they got, the more rebellious they became and wouldn't take kindly to women giving them orders. Once they reached that rebellious age he'd cut 'em off but if they were good he'd put them to work outside of Emerald City. He wanted as little distractions for us as possible. I respected his plan but Yvette didn't give a fuck. She was ready to handle them no matter how damn old they were. And most, if not all of the soldiers *feared* or *respected* Yvette. She could handle shit with the best of men.

While Yvette was briefing the soldiers the others turned around and saw me standing there not dressed for the occasion or the night.

"What you doin'? Why ain't you dressed?" Kenyetta asked, as she looked me up and down.

I had to give it to my girl, she was killing a red dress, Fendi heels with the red and black lace mink Fendi purse to match it. Kenyetta was 5'7 with dark pretty skin and Indian hair that fell to the middle of her back. Tonight she had it up in a classy bun. Men killed for Kenyetta but she belonged to Dyson, one of the members of the Emerald City squad.

"Yeah…what's up wit' that, Cedes'?" Yvette asked after finishing with the workers who were now at the bottom of the steps manning the gates. "Go put your shit on. Dex and Stacy will be here in a minute," she continued as she pulled out her compact to check her lipstick.

Yvette wasn't the prettiest but with the money she earned and the power she had, she quickly became one of the most wanted women in the projects, along with the rest of us. She was a shorty with big titties and a phat ass to go with it. We joked all the time about her being one sandwich away from being overweight. She hadn't always been that way. I guess running Emerald City's gates and leading the soldiers took its toll on her body. She had a smooth amber complexion, and sported a short spiky haircut. Her hair, was always fierce regardless of what she had going on.

At 5'5 inches, she was the meanest bitch you could ever come across. I gave the soldiers leeway on *certain* shit but Yvette didn't give them any on anything. She was in charge of security and made it clear that she wasn't the one to be fucked with, skirt or not. She would carry any nigga anywhere if the money was fucked up or if they were caught slippin'. Being the baddest bitch, it was only fitting that she fucked with the meanest nigga of the Emerald City Squad. And Thick was the only man who could handle her.

When he came into the room, you couldn't help but respect him. Even the scar on his face made you wonder about the life he led.

"Don't start with me. I'm mad enough as it is," I said brushing off their comments. I wasn't in the mood to go into what happened with my two-faced mother.

"Don't start with you?! Bitch tonight is our night! This is the only night we get recognized for the shit we go through in EC! Ain't no otha' project being held down by bitches outside of Emerald!" Carissa insisted.

Carissa was usually laid back, but not when she felt passionate about something. She looked just like a young Salli Richardson only better. Her skin was copper-colored and she didn't have a flaw on her body. Not even a mole. She wore her hair in a jazzy bob, which brushed her cheeks every time she moved. She was beautiful.

The niggas gave her the most shit because she was short and cute and when they saw her, all they thought about was fuckin'. But just like we all dealt with members of the Emerald City squad, Carissa was no exception because she was messing with Lavelle. And the niggas around here knew if anybody loved their woman, he did. He wouldn't have a problem putting two to any of these nigga's head who disrespected him or her.

"Go get dressed!" Yvette insisted. "Stacy just called and said she'll be out front in a minute. They comin' through the gate now."

"I can't roll ya'll. I'm serious," I said tucking my hands back inside my warm pockets. "My mother can't watch the kids tonight."

"Please say you playin'!" Yvette yelled. "Damn! Call her I'll see if she'll do it for me."

"Don't waste your time. I tried offering her four large and she still said no."

"So you ain't playin?" Yvette asked in disbelief.

"Naw, I'm not playin, but I wish I was. She messing with Mr. Brown again and she think I don't know that shit. You know his wife's out of town this week at that Mary Kay convention."

"Mom's wrong as shit," Kenyetta said shaking her head.

"Tell me about it. But ya'll go ahead. Just tell me how it was," I said, trying to hide the fact that I really didn't want them to go without me. We did everything together. And I wanted to see if they would ride or die with me for real.

"Look...why don't you let Tina watch 'em?" Yvette asked.

She already knew the answer to that, so I don't even know why she let if fall out of her mouth.

Tina and her badass kids lived with Yvette from time to time when her mother who lived across the hallway put her out. Regardless there was no way in hell I was letting her watch my kids. Besides, Yvette's apartment was nasty and too junky for my taste. The last time I let Crystal stay over Yvette's she came back with bumps all over her arms and face. I think they were roach bites and I was mad as shit with Yvette. I got over it after awhile but I made a promise that it would never happen again. Yvette's my girl but she could take better care of her crib. I'm surprised Thick's big ass ain't put her in her place yet.

"Naw. I can't do that. You know I like L'il C to be at his own house, around his own things."

"You spoil those kids rotten!" Kenyetta said. "And L'il C damn near runnin' the place." She giggled.

Before we could get into anything else, Stacia and Dex pulled up in front of the building in his silver Hummer. Stacia looked beautiful. Her white fur coat was the first thing I saw before her glossy lips started moving.

"Party night!" she screamed through the open window.

"No she didn't get the white mink I wanted!" Carissa said. "Dex stay lacing her up!"

"I know don't she look beautiful?" I added, trying to hide the fact that I was slightly jealous.

The cold air blowing through the window pushed her long hair into her face and teased her fur coat. Her honey brown skin was flawless. She was so beautiful that no one questioned why Dex chose her. We walked down the steps and by the soldiers who were already guarding Emerald city.

"Hey baby!" I said as Stacia jumped out and gave us all hugs.

"Hey you!" Stacia yelled back.

Dex came around to the passenger side to open the doors for us and we hugged him too. Stacia and Dex was livin' it up for real. They were the Beyoncé and Jay-Z of Emerald City and we adored them. Their relationship was the example we used when we talked to our men. They all made promises to move us out of Emerald City once we got things tight, but Dex kept his promise to Stacia.

They use to live here in Emerald City with us until he became the Chief in command and started pulling in six-figures a month. Although Dex got put on and eventually moved, he didn't stop showin' love to the rest of us.

He was here so much we started forgetting he even moved to Alexandria, Virginia with Stacia in their eight-bedroom castle style home.

Dex showed his loyalty, but Stacia was another story. She used to come by all the time to sit with us on the steps of Unit C, like we did before they moved from the projects. We could talk to her about anything. From our relationships to our dreams. And if Stacia could make it happen or help us, she would. She always had the answers. When she left it kinda hurt. Our group had been dismantled and it hurt even more when she stopped coming around as much. But when Dex started getting kidnap threats about Stacia, he told her to cut the visits short.

Sometimes she didn't listen. She'd just dress down so people wouldn't recognize her if they saw her sitting with us. But the moment anybody saw the fifth girl posted up in front of Unit C, they'd know exactly who she was no matter how she tried to disguise herself. We all missed Stacia but understood that Dex kept his promise, and we wanted her to be happy.

Dex didn't always have it that way. At one point, he ran hand and hand with my boyfriend Cameron, Dyson, Thick and Lavelle. But after Dreyfus, our supplier came in blasting on Tyland Towers, a project a few blocks over from ours, Dex came up with a plan that sealed his position as the man of Emerald city.

They say Dreyfus is 6'3 dark-skinned with smooth black

hair. But no matter what he looked like, he was ruthless. He didn't get involved with every little detail that happened in the projects and hated being bothered with bullshit. The only thing he demanded was his money be right and on time, *every time*. About three years ago, The Tyland Towers crew failed to heed his warning.

When some stick up kids from uptown D.C got the inside scoop from somebody on the inside as to where the warehouse was in Tyland Towers they took full advantage. They got into the Tyland Tower crew for over two hundred thousand dollars in cash and product that night. And all of that shit was on consignment. When Dreyfus found out that Jamal, who ran Tyland Towers, let some niggas get into him for that much cash, he came through with ten niggas on Thanksgiving Day blastin'.

He killed off all of Jamal's troops and sliced his throat in front of his pregnant girlfriend Patricia. Then he called a meeting with all the captains from all the spots he supplied. Dex went to represent Emerald City because there was no lieutenant at that time. While they were there, Dreyfus reminded them of his policies, particularly not having his money fucked with, using Tyland Towers as an example. He vowed that shit would be worse if it happened again.

After the meeting, Dex came up with the idea of the gatekeepers. He called Cameron, Dyson, Thick and Lavelle, also known as the Emerald City Squad and told them about his plan. Instead of them hating, they put the plan in action to ensure what happened to Tyland Towers didn't happen to Emerald City.

The plan consisted of four gatekeepers running the largest unit, Unit C, at all times. Since all of Emerald City could clearly be seen from Unit C, one responsibility of a gatekeeper's was to handle 'the approach'.

The approach happened the moment the security gave the wave that something wasn't right with whoever was coming through. Two people handled that function. The other person handled security and the fourth handled the collection of the funds.

Dex's plan worked so well, that Dreyfus made him Chief of Emerald City. But when the money really started flowing, it became difficult for the EC squad to man the gates alone. More fiends were coming through which meant more product and more responsibility. They hadn't anticipated what would happen if things worked out so well, and because of it, they never trained anyone else on the Gatekeeper plan because they didn't trust anyone.

That's when Thick came up with the plan to put us out there. Since we were around them all the time, they trusted us and we knew Emerald City inside out. That was three years ago, and we've been manning the gate ever since.

"Wow girl, you wearing jeans?" Stacia asked tugging at the loop on my belt. "That's different."

"I'm not wearing jeans...I can't go," I said, avoiding the disappointment on my friend's face.

"What? Why?!" she asked looking at Dex, who looked more and more like money every time I saw him. The diamond earring in his right ear was so bright it almost looked like a flashlight.

"Damn girl! Does your man know that? I just saw him and he ain't say shit about that," Dex asked with his raspy voice.

"Not yet, I can't find him anywhere. You know how ya'll take all day to get ready for the ball. He put more time into tonight than he did on me." I laughed. "Well look, go ahead and have fun!" I didn't want to continue to throw a pity party outside of Unit C and bring everyone down. "I'll be a'ight."

"We can't leave you," Yvette said. "You know that shit.

How we gonna go to the Hustler's Ball with one of the Gatekeepers missin'?"

"But ya'll look so nice. Seriously, y'all can go without me." I really wanted them to stay and chill with me but I knew how bad they wanted to show off their outfits.

"Naw....we chillin' wit' you tonight!" Kenyetta said as she hit my arm. "But damn girl, I was gonna kill them in this dress tonight!" She pouted. "Dyson woulda been mad at my ass when I came through them doors. He needs to be thankin' you," she continued as she opened her fur coat revealing her red dress. I could tell that if you shined the right light on it, you would've been able to see right through it.

"You? I wanted to show mine off too!" Carissa opened her coat revealing her short black Missoni dress under her fur coat, which cost over two grand. "They wasn't gonna be ready for what I was gonna give."

"Well since we're having a fashion show," Yvette said. "I was gonna kill 'em in my dress too." Yvette's white on white look made her look sexy and sophisticated. The full-length fur coat set off her Emilio Pucci dress gracefully. They all looked like a million bucks. And for what? To stay home. "Anyway...go ahead Stacia. We'll see you later."

"Well okay guys!" Stacia sighed. "I hope ya'll know you're breakin' my heart. How you gonna leave me with the guys alone?"

"You can handle 'em." Carissa laughed. "And keep a close eye on my man."

"I'll try," she laughed back. "I'm gonna call ya'll tomorrow!" Stacia said as Dex hugged us then opened the door for her. "Don't forget about the cookout and bring my babies! *All* of them Mercedes!"

"Okay...I will." I waved.

"I have a surprise for them too." She continued as she

jumped in the truck and Dex got behind the wheel. "I love ya'll!"

"We love you too! Have fun!" We waved as they drove to the party.

"Sorry ya'll. I know how bad you guys wanted to go," I said, happy they decided to stay. I figured the least I could do was get them high. "Well since we got the soldiers at the gates tonight, let's crack open the Ace of Spades I have in my apartment on chill. Plus Big Cameron left me a phat ass J too," I continued as we walked up the steps.

"I'm wit' that shit!" Carissa said smiling.

"Me too." Yvette added, linking her arm with Kenyetta's. "As long as we got each other, I'm good."

Even though we didn't make it to the ball, we still had a nice time laughing and talking about old times.

We were still up at four a.m. when the phone rang. No one expected to hear what we did when I answered the phone. And the news would change our lives forever.

CHAPTER 2
BURYING FRIENDS
DECEMBER, WEDNESDAY, 10:37 A.M.

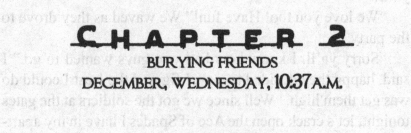

YVETTE

It was the worst day of all our lives.

We were watching our men carrying the caskets of Stacia and Dex, walking them to the hearse that would later take them to the place they would be buried. Everyone was still in shock, mainly because of how they were killed. The way it went down was scandalous. Someone had hid in the back of Dex's truck, escaping detection by the gatekeepers. Whoever did it knew that no one would be inspecting Dex's truck and used that to their advantage. It was against *our* law to inspect a squad member's car or stop them at the gate.

They sliced Stacia's pretty face over thirty times before stabbing her in the stomach. And what they did to Dex was unreal. Those muthafuckas actually partially severed his head from his body. They stole all their jewelry including the diamond earring that Dex bought the moment he became the man of Emerald City. But they didn't just take the diamond out, they ripped his ear off. Because of how they did them, we all knew it wasn't just a robbery. The shit was personal, but no one knew why. Dex and Stacia were rich, but they were good people, helping anybody they could.

Through it all, I couldn't shake the fact that if we

would've gotten into his truck the night of the ball, they would've been burying all six of us.

L'il C not watching the kids had probably been the best thing that could've happened to us. I'm happy Mercedes ain't believe in breaking promises to her son.

There were so many people paying their respects that we had to relive the funeral four times that day just to allow everyone a chance to say goodbye. All you saw were dudes dressed in jeans, white T-shirts, Timb's and blazers. There were flower arrangements everywhere including one in the shape of Emerald City, Dex's Hummer and every kind of gun imaginable. Two gold framed pictures of Dex and Stacia faced the crowd.

The girls and I did our best to hold it together until the last funeral session. Due to the way they had been killed, all of the services were closed casket. Hearing and seeing how differently people felt about two people we considered family, punched us in our stomach every time. With every tear shed, and cry heard, we were broken down. It was like we were soaking up their pain, and trying to find a place for it in our hearts.

Our men did what they could to console us, but they were going through it too. But being tough like they were, they wouldn't allow it to show. There were too many people there, most of which they didn't want to face later if they were seen crying.

I couldn't help but feel responsible. And although no one said anything to me yet, I felt *fully* responsible. I knew that eventually I would have to answer on how they got through

Emerald City's gates undetected the night of the Hustler's ball. *I was in charge! Shit! Why didn't I just go back out on post instead of drinking?* I just hoped that Thick wasn't angry with me. I hated letting him down.

"You okay baby? Don't worry 'bout this shit! We handlin' it!" Thick said as he pulled me to his crisp black suit and squeezed me tight.

There was nothing better than his strong hugs and deep dark voice to soothe me. I wanted him, right now. He made me feel safe. Suddenly I felt bad for being turned on considering we had just buried our friends, but I couldn't help myself. I loved everything about him. Especially the feel of his thick dick when he moved in and out of my body, the way he fussed at me when he felt I was being weak and the way he always came to my rescue, when I needed him. I couldn't wait until we spent our lives together, and he kept his promise to pull me out of Emerald City for good. And I was patiently waiting.

"I'm fine. I want you to know that I'm gonna find out who did this Thick." I told him as he released me to look into my eyes. He wiped the tears off my face with his large rough hand.

He looked down on me and said, "Baby? What you talkin' 'bout? Me and my niggas got this! We know this ain't have shit to do wit' you holdin' shit down in the EC. I just want you to be a'ight so you can do what needs to be done tomorrow. Shit is gonna be business as usual in the city, and we still have an operation to run."

"But this is my fault."

"Yvette!" he said, grabbing my shoulders. "Don't worry 'bout this shit, I got this! Believe dat! I need you to keep focused. If them mothafuckas woulda merked me I would've expected you to be tough and be on post the next day. This is business."

The thought of losing him *ever*, hurt.

Thick leaned in and kissed me. My body melted into his as I inhaled his scent.

"You comin' home tonight baby? I mean....I know you been busy and all, but I really miss you."

"I'll try baby," he said softly. "But you know wit' shit bein' tight now, me and the nigga's gotta handle all of Dex's business and collect debt from a few folks who owe him. *Truthfully*, Daddy may not be able to play house for a little while."

My heart dropped and I tried my best to hide my disappointment. But lately Thick hadn't been coming home like he use to. I felt bad for reaching for his attention, using the death of my friends as a reason, but I needed him home. I tried everything I could think of to make him come home more often. I fixed his favorite meals, cleaned up the house when I could and even stopped fussing at him 'bout dumb shit, but nothing seemed to work.

We had been living together in Emerald City for six years, but over the past year he'd stay with me once a week if that. As far as I knew, he didn't have another place, so I hated thinking about where he was staying. Whenever I asked him, he'd tell me he was in and out of New York handling business so he'd stay in hotels. I hoped it was true, but I knew in my heart it wasn't.

I rubbed my hand over the scar left on his face from the car accident a few years back. For some reason it turned me on even more. His chocolate covered skin and 6'4 inch body earned him the name Thick.

"I understand baby. But don't forget about me... *Please* don't forget about me."

"How can I forget about you Yvette? You know that shit

ain't possible, but I need you to be strong."

"I'm tryin' to be strong for you Thick, but I don't know how much more I can take in EC I want to be with you. I'm ready."

"You know now is not a good time baby." He sighed and his voice was heavy with irritation.

"I know Thick, but me and the girls been training niggas on the side, so we can be ready to leave when shit finally takes off for us."

"Don't tell me you can't handle shit!" His voice was deep and his facial expression changed. I could tell he didn't like the idea of me preparing without him.

"I *can* handle it baby but-."

"I know you can," he cut me off. "You wouldn't be out there if you couldn't handle shit."

A few people turned around and looked at us. That's when I remembered we were at Stacia and Dex's house having the repass. Just that quickly I had gotten lost in Thick and our conversation. I missed him so much that anytime he gave me attention, I sucked up as much of it as I could. I wanted every part of it, and if that was wrong, right now, I didn't even care.

"Listen baby. I'ma get you out of Emerald, but you gotta give me some more time. The only reason shit was easy for Dex, was because he impressed Dreyfus wit' the gatekeeper plan.

"We still livin' off his fame right now and unless we come up wit' somethin' different, all we doin' is seein' plenty of money but keepin' none of it. Just stay wit' me baby. Shit gonna be a'ight, and then we gonna get that big house we talked about," he said as he reached in for one last kiss before he walked away, taking my heart with him.

I saw Mercedes and them with their men and I wondered if they were feeding them the same thing Thick fed me, and most of all, if they believed it. The only reason we were strong enough to hold Emerald City down was because of them and if we didn't have them, we ain't want no part of it, and that was the truth.

I scanned the room and watched grief dwell among the crowd. Slowly the gathering was turning from a somber event to one where people were beginning to find joy in the memories of Dex and Stacia. Just when I thought that things just might be okay, what I saw next ripped my heart to pieces.

Thick was hugging a girl I had never seen before, at least around the hood anyway. He was consoling her, right in front of me.

Curiosity was killing me and I wanted to walk across the room and demand that he tell me what the fuck was up, but I couldn't say anything because if she was a family member of Stacia or Dex, I would feel worse than I already did.

The only thing that kept entering my mind was that we all knew the same people. Our family was large, but our inner circle was tight. If she were somebody worth knowing, I would've known her.

I tried to brush it off but the more I did the angrier I grew inside. Something was up.

CHAPTER 3

BUSINESS AS USUAL
DECEMBER, THURSDAY, 5:45 P.M.

KENYETTA

"You got some more Doritos?" I asked Yvette.

"No girl. I killed them shits a long time ago!" Yvette said.

"Why you would even ask that girl if she had anymore is what I want to know." Mercedes laughed.

"And what the fuck is that supposed to mean?" Yvette said as she stood up from one of the four grey metal chairs that we kept outside. "I just finished 'em."

"Yeah right!" Carissa stuck her hands in her pockets and tried to stay as warm as the rest of us. "You sucked them down the moment you broke the seal. Everybody know you don't be sharin' no food!" Everyone laughed.

This was the life for us. We were sitting on the top step watching over Emerald City and the gate. Seven days a week. People made me mad when they said hustlers didn't *earn* their money, and they were just stealing from a weaker group of people. That's bullshit. I wonder if those same muthafuc-ka could stand outside and freeze their asses off for twelve hours a day, and *still* look as good as we did.

I mean we were charged with everything. With making our men happy, with looking good at all times which meant keeping our hair appointments, and wearing fly shit. And most of all, we were charged with being in charge of over sixty nigga's, who had a problem with answering to women.

"I miss them ya'll. I can't act like it didn't happen anymore," Mercedes said as she looked at us from under the peach hat she wore with her peach Baby Phat ski coat.

Mercedes was beautiful. Her vanilla colored complexion and black hair brought out her big pretty eyes.

"Me too... I don't understand this shit. Dex was paid and all, but he would've put anybody on if they would've proven themselves!" Carissa said as she tied her black scarf around her neck and adjusted her black full-length Eddie Bauer coat. It was obvious she wasn't playing with this cold ass air, while the rest of us were pressed to look colorful and cute.

"Well I'ma see if Dramon and them seen anything. I knew we should've stayed out here the moment Mercedes couldn't get a sitter! That was some type of omen or something. That was the sign we needed to check shit out a little further but we didn't. We all know that we never miss a ball, so why all of a sudden did Aunt Linda say she couldn't watch the kids? I'm tellin' yall it was a sign!"

"No it wasn't. My freak ass mother just wanted to fuck wit' Mr. Brown that's why we couldn't go," Mercedes added.

"That maybe true but that wasn't all," Yvette continued. "We shoulda looked into shit a little further I'm telling ya'll!"

Everybody knew that Yvette had been beating herself up over what happened to them. We all knew she was in charge of security, but she wasn't alone. We all stood right outside that truck and none of us saw those niggas in the back. We knew it wasn't her fault but being the perfectionist she was you couldn't tell her that.

"We could've looked into things all day long," I said. "But we would've never seen that shit coming....Never!"

We were silent for the next few minutes, and I took from

that that everyone agreed with me. Dex and Stacia being murdered had taken a serious toll on the atmosphere in Emerald City. For a long time, shit would be real fucked up around here. I just knew it.

"We don't give a fuck! If you comin' through here, we wanna know where the fuck you goin'!" I said to two girls driving in a green Honda Accord, trying to enter the gate.

The guards hit me on my Nextel and said there was a problem the moment they tried to pull through. They weren't trying to cooperate by giving them the additional information we requested before entering through the gates. Technically all they *really* had to do was give them the apartment and building number. But the EC squad wanted the name and affiliation but these bitches weren't trying to give it to them, so as far as we were concerned, they weren't getting through, especially after what happened to Dex and Stacia. Security was *extra* tight in the city.

"Bitch who the fuck you talkin' too? I'm comin' here to see my man, and I ain't got to tell you his name, or where the fuck he live!" The fat one yelled from the passenger seat.

"Listen, we ain't tryin' to give you a hard time, but if you wanna come through Emerald City's gates, you *have* to tell us where the fuck you goin' or else you ain't gettin' in! It's as simple as that," Carissa said standing on the passenger side of the car.

"Oh I know you, you fuck wit' Lavelle," the light skinned girl said to Carissa, from the driver's seat.

"And? What the fuck that got to do with why you here?" She shot back.

"Nothin…it ain't got nothing to do wit' it for real for real. I just thought you oughta know that I know Lavelle," she said laughing a little, like the joke was on Carissa.

"Why the fuck I oughta know that? That ain't got shit to do with you gettin' in this muthafucka!" Carissa yelled.

That's my girl! Don't let them bitches know you're moved.

"Listen bitches, either tell us where the fuck you goin or turn this raggedy ass car around! Right now the choice is yours, but if you keep running your fuckin' mouths, I can't promise you will get to leave this bitch unharmed."

They looked at each other realizing we weren't playing. Just because she tried to disrespect Carissa, I was more than ready to pull her out of the car and pay Shaneta and them across the field $50 to stomp the fuck out of these bitches, until *Carissa* said stop.

"OK…calm down. We got it," the driver said sarcastically. "Tell them where we goin' girl, after all, we do know Lavelle and he's cool. He *real* cool. I don't want him thinkin' we tried to play his l'il girlfriend," she continued, looking up at Carissa grinning.

All I was thinking was that if Yvette had been in charge of the approach instead of security she would've knocked this bitch in her face the moment she said Lavelle's name out of her mouth. Just on G.P alone.

"Well…*anyway*. I'm goin' to see Derrick in Unit C. He's expectin' me. You can call him right now if you don't believe me," the passenger said.

"Naw…it's cool. But next time just say that shit," I said, giving the security guards the signal to let them in. I should've known these dumb ass bitches were coming to see Derrick's troublemaking ass. "And stop wasting everybody's fucking time!"

As they pulled off and parked in the lot on the side of Unit

C, I wondered what was up with that. What had me messed up the most was the fact they knew Derrick. It seemed to me that he should've warned his bitches about Emerald City's policies but apparently, he didn't. I knew that Derrick constantly tried Mercedes, and that he had no respect for women in authority. I also knew that eventually we'd have to deal with him before shit hit the fan.

The other thing that was wild was how she kept reppin' Lavelle's name like she *really* knew him or something. I knew that the moment our shift was over, Carissa would be deep in Lavelle's shit, and I didn't blame her.

The moment Dyson called me and said he would be over; I finished my shift an hour early and drove to my apartment in Unit B.

But when he walked through the door, he slumped on the couch and didn't appear to be in the same lovemaking mood I was.

"Listen Kenyetta, y'all gonna have to watch everything around here," he said. "With Dex gone a lot of niggas are gonna try us, thinkin' we ain't got shit tight no more. We gonna be comin' around more to make our presence known, but don't be caught slippin'. Ya'll have to really watch each othas backs."

"And what about the dope testers? We still runnin' them next week?"

"Yeah…But make sure niggas play it smooth. I don't trust nobody. I can't believe they took my man! Damn!" he said, as he rubbing the side of his head.

"I know baby, I miss him and Stacia too."

"This shit is fucked up! Why they had to fuck with Dex? He wasn't even that type of dude." He was trying to hold his tears back by screaming, but it wasn't working. And I was ready to be there to kiss each one that he let fall.

"Don't worry, we got our hands in everything. We ain't lettin' shit slide by baby," I said trying to reassure him.

"I know you do baby, but I'm serious. Beware of everybody and everything. With us giving them testers out this week, the gates are gonna be flooded with fiends. We need to make sure everybody's on the up and up."

Dyson was serious and it scared me a little. Prior to now he never acted as if he doubted we had things under control. What hurt the most was that although I missed him and needed him to hold me; he was briefing me like I was a soldier and not his lady.

"Okay baby," I said as I grabbed his hands. "But tonight I need you. I need to be with you. Can you just make love to me?"

He smiled and pulled me down on the couch with him. I had gotten rid of my grandmother earlier and was happy to be spending some quality time *alone* with my man. Lately she had been getting too nosey and asking too many questions. She wanted to know who was looking over this unit, and who was looking over that unit, instead of worrying about her high blood pressure and taking care of her health.

He took off his jacket and I knelt down and removed his shoes. When both were off, I slid off his jeans exposing his crisp white boxers and rising dick. It was just the confirmation I needed, to know that he wanted me.

I slowly lifted up his shirt while kissing him softly on his chest. Then I made my way to his lips and gently sucked them.

"What you doin' to me girl?" he moaned.

"I'm making love to my man," I told him seductively.

Before going any further, I removed his boxers and reminded him of how vicious my head game was. Slowly and softly, I sucked his dick as if my life depended on it. He ran his fingers through my hair while thrusting softly in my mouth. I knew that no matter what, my sex game could always bring him back to me. At least I hoped.

That night I fucked him in every way he wanted. Dyson had told me that it was my sex game that hooked him, but it was my heart that kept him. Although I loved that he appreciated how good I could make him feel, I battled with the idea that another girl could be out there doing the same thing to him, if not better. So I vowed that whenever I made love to Dyson, I would fuck him as if it was the first time, every time. Because in my heart…it was.

CHAPTER 4
ADDED DRAMA
DECEMBER, FRIDAY, 10:38 P.M.

CARISSA

"I can't believe you ain't giving Lavelle none of that backdoor action!" Yvette laughed with the rest of our friends. "You better take care of your man girl, before somebody else does."

"I do take care of him, but ain't nothing wrong with my pussy either," I told her.

"I can't believe you don't like takin' it in the ass, Carissa," Mercedes laughed as she drank from the Hennessey and Coke mixture in her cup.

"That shit is too uncomfortable for me. I told his ass the last time he asked me not to ask me again."

"You wild as shit!" Yvette laughed.

"He ain't complaining though. Trust me."

"I told you what to do, Carissa. You have to put some bomb ass music on, get the K.Y Jelly, and tell Lavelle to ease it in *slowly*. You can't rush a dick into virgin ass. You have to be easy wit' it," Mercedes added.

"Naw. I tried that and it *still* didn't work. I ain't fuckin' with y'all no more. Messin' with y'all the last time, I got my asshole damn near ripped out."

"Trust me, you'll be lovin' that shit before the night is

29

over," Mercedes laughed as she gave the others five.

I couldn't believe my friends were letting their men hit it from the back. They loved ragging on me about how I sexed Lavelle but he complimented me all the time on the way I handled him in the bedroom. As far as I was concerned, if their men had to fuck them in the ass, something was wrong with them, not me.

We all stopped talking when Critter, the most trusted dope head in the hood came running up the steps. Although we liked him, we never allowed anybody to approach us unless it was a resident going into the building, or one of the lieutenants. We stood up and all put our hands on our guns. We trusted Critter but after what happened to Dex and Stacia, we couldn't give out benefits of the doubt no more. For all we knew somebody could've given him a bag of dope to smoke us all.

"What up Critter? You know you ain't supposed to come up here like that," Yvette reminded him with her hand tucked in her coat, holding her weapon.

"I know...I know...but Derrick won't give me a tester!" he said. He looked bad. The effect the withdrawals were having on his body was evident.

I asked him, "What you talkin' 'bout, Critter?"

"Me and Rod went up to him to cop a piece. He gives him three, and turns around and tells me to get the fuck outta his face."

"Why he say that?" Mercedes asked.

"He said I got one already."

"So just get one from Rod!" I told him, trying to prevent what I knew was getting ready to happen, which was more drama with Derrick's ass.

"I tried to ask him, but Rod took off running the moment Derrick hooked him up. Ya'll know you can't catch no fiend," he laughed trying to make a quick joke. "Can you please talk to him for me? I ain't feelin' too good."

We all knew why Derrick did that shit to him but he was being real petty, because although it wasn't the law, he was supposed to be servicing *all* of our customers. Not just the ones he liked, or better yet, the ones that looked out for us.

Critter was valuable to us when it came to getting the word out to other fiends when we had new product. He was our eyes and ears in places we couldn't or wouldn't dare go to, and because of it Derrick couldn't stand him.

"Don't worry 'bout it, Critter. We got you," Kenyetta said turning her attention toward the soldier at the bottom of the stairs. "Hey, DJ! Come up here for a sec." DJ ran up the steps to see what was up.

"What up, Vette? Want me to carry his ass outta of here?"

"Naw he cool. You got anymore testers on you?"

"Yeah I got a few."

"Well hook Critter up, and if you see Derrick, tell him we want to talk to him for a minute."

"Cool. Come on, Critter. I'll give it to you down there." DJ new better than to exchange drugs in our presence and he was following procedure. We didn't want to ever get caught with dope on or around us and run the risk of being locked up. That would put the entire operation in jeopardy.

"Thanks ya'll." Critter said. "I 'preciate this and if ya'll need me to wash your cars tomorrow, bring 'em 'round front."

"It's cold as shit out here, Critter," Yvette laughed. "Just get us next time or somethin'."

"You got it!" He continued running down the steps.

Derrick was becoming a pain. He couldn't seem to understand that things were the way that they were, and there was nothing he could do about it. It was better to go with the flow, then to go against it. He did everything we told him to, but in his own way and in his own time and frankly, he was getting on my fuckin' nerves.

When Derrick walked up the stairs, he already looked like he was gonna give us trouble. His face was twisted with aggravation.

"Derrick...why you fuckin' wit' Critter? You know he brings us a lot of business around here," Mercedes asked shoving her hands in her pockets.

"I ain't fuckin' wit' him. I thought he already had one and I wasn't givin' him another one."

"Look, Derrick, stop fuckin' with him. Treat him the fuck like you treat everybody else!" Mercedes yelled. "He a customer just like these otha muthafuckas out here."

"Man what you want me to do? Give him whatever he wants whenever he asks for it? We won't neva make no damn money fuckin' wit' his ass."

"That ain't what she saying, Derrick. She saying stop giving people who you know look out for Emerald City bullshit," Yvette was about to get in his shit for the disrespect. If he said one more word, he could possibly be cut off. "And since you here, what's up with them girls you had comin' through here yesterday? They almost got fucked up for real."

"Man that's my girl! What you sayin? Ya'll controlling who I fuck wit' too?" he asked, obviously upset.

"We ain't sayin' that shit. What we telling you is to control your bitches!" I screamed. "Now if you fuck wit' her like you say you do, I'm sure you want her breathing."

"Whatever."

"Yeah what the fuck ever! Get back to work nigga."

He looked back at me like he wanted to kill me, and as far as I was concerned, if he wanted to bring it, I was ready. With Yvette and my girls backing me, he would have a hard time.

The bottom line was, I was tired of his blatant disrespect to everything we said to him. He wasn't runnin' Emerald City, we were! I made a mental note to tell Lavelle to cut his ass off the moment I talked to him cuz I'm tired of his shit.

One of our lieutenants from Unit A, Doctanian, came up the steps. "Carissa, we 569."

That meant they were low on supply, and because shop wasn't closed for another three hours, we had to replenish him. There are three stash houses in EC, one in every building. Since I was going home anyway, and lived in Unit A myself, I decided to hook him up.

"I'll handle it ya'll." I told them as I zipped my coat and ran down the stairs to my car.

"You want one of the soldiers to go with you?" Yvette asked.

"Naw I'm good. Anyway, you know the rules. They can't know where the stash house is so I'll be a'ight," I told them as I walked toward the building.

"You got anything on you now?" I asked Doctanian as I approached the door to Unit A.

"Yeah we got a little something, but for real we butt naked as shit out here!" he said as he served a head, who was mad that he'd taken a few seconds to give me the status.

"I got you," I told him as I went inside.

Once in the hallway I made sure no one followed me, or noticed me heading toward the stash house. We made it a point to change them up on the regular to keep people off our track, and prevent niggas from robbing us like they did a few years back at Tyland Towers. When I saw the coast was clear,

I walked toward the elevator and pushed the button for the fourth floor.

Kristina ran the stash house for Unit A, and only eight people had the key. Originally, it was only the Emerald City Squad but since they were away a lot running other shops, they had four keys made for us too. Besides the eight of us, only Dreyfus, Dex and Kristina, who had been working with him for years, knew were we kept our product.

When I opened the door to A46, Kristina who was 60 years old and had been in the game all her life, stood up and held the end of the gun she carried in the holster. Her fine thinning hair was pulled tightly into a ponytail, and she had a cigarette in her mouth like she always did every time I saw her. The apartment looked just like a factory. There were boxes and boxes of empty vials, rolls of glassine paper, and money wrappers everywhere. The other two stash houses looked similar in Emerald City, and were ran by other loyal workers too. She managed all of them but only worked the one in Unit A.

"It's just me." I quickly told her before she let one loose from her gun.

"Oh…Carissa. What you here for? They low already out there?" she asked as she sat down.

"Yeah…I need to get a little bit of everything. We closing shop in a few hours anyway, but they still need somethin' right now. The testers killed us today cuz they were buying two and gettin' one free."

"If they smart they would," she said as she put out her cigarette, and moved toward the packaged supplies.

When she handed me enough dope, crack, weed and E pills to last them a few hours, I chilled for a while to make sure no one was on my trail. When I felt I waited long enough, I stuffed the product in the inside of my Eddie Bauer coat, and looked out the peephole before opening the door.

I was halfway to the elevators when I saw three figures in dark clothes with their hoodies pulled over their heads quickly moving in my direction.

"There she go right there!" One of them whispered as they ran toward me. "Get that bitch!"

I know this ain't happening! I can't believe somebody would be bold enough to rob me. They had to have a death wish. With my heart in my throat, I took off in the opposite direction knowing that it would eventually lead me to the other side of the floor by another elevator. The coat was weighing me down, but I moved as fast as I could. I was willing to bust my gun if I had to, and was prepared to take as many of them with me as possible.

One of them yelled as the other took off in the opposite direction. "One of ya'll go the other way, so we can catch that bitch in the middle!"

Now what was I gonna do? They were trying to block me in. Constantly checking my back, I was running fast enough to put a nice amount of space in between us. The faster I ran, the more I moved out of their sight. I noticed the janitor's closet but didn't go in right away. I wanted them to think I went down the stairwell so I opened the door and slammed it. Then I turned the knob to the closet and prayed that the door was open. It was!

I quickly but quietly squeezed myself into the closet, and locked the door behind me. Here I was in a closet with over $1000 dollars worth of shit in my pockets. I knew if they tried to open the door, I'd be dead. And if they decided to fill the closet with led, there would be nowhere I could run. There was hardly anywhere in the closet for me to move. Not to mention, the smell of the mop bucket filled with soiled water next to me reeked of piss and Pine-Sol mixed.

I tried desperately to stop my heavy breathing, and hoped they would think I went down the stairway, which was through the door directly across from me. When they stopped in front of the closet, I was scared. I covered my mouth when my teeth began to rattle. *Please God get me out of this.* I could see them a little through the slots in the door, but not clearly. Completely out of breath due to chasing me, they talked in low voices.

"Where…you…think she went?"

"I heard her run out the door! I hope she ain't see our faces," the other said.

I tried to see them, but from where I sat, no one looked familiar. The slots blurred their faces. Maybe it was the adrenaline, but my mind was completely messed up. By this time the other guy who ran in the opposite direction reached them.

"Where she at?!" he asked out of breath.

"We don't fuckin' know."

"Well let's get out of here before she tells them Emerald City niggas! Damn! We should've waited for her to come to the elevators!"

"We can't worry 'bout that shit now. Let's roll!" They said before running down the stairway.

I sat in the closet for ten more minutes before moving. I waited until their footsteps completely faded. When the were gone, I called the first person I thought of…Lavelle.

"Baby!" I said in between my tears. "I was set up. Some nigga's just tried to rob me."

"I'm on my way!" Lavelle yelled through the phone.

Shit was about to get real deadly in Emerald City. I just knew it.

CHAPTER 5

THE EMERALD CITY SQUAD
DECEMBER, FRIDAY, 11:45 P.M.

The passengers in the Black Ford Excursion 4X2 XLS were completely silent.

Lavelle, Thick, Dyson and Cameron were all inside, as the sounds of "Hail Mary" filled the air as if Tupac himself was riding with them. They already discussed the robbery situation at Thick's slides house. Thick's slide was a broad out in B-More that he fucked on the side. They expected niggas to try something sooner or later, but they didn't expect it to happen this soon. And they never expected one of the girls to be the target.

"I'm tellin' ya'll, if they would've hurt Carissa...I'dda lit that whole muthafucka up!" Lavelle said breaking the silence.

"I feel you son, but don't worry 'bout shit, we gonna handle them muthafuckas," Cameron promised.

Lavelle was crushed. He would've murdered everybody in Unit A if something had happened to Carissa. The thought of almost losing her was causing him to lose his temper. Out of all the squad he loved his girl the most. He meant what he said when he told her the moment the money was good, and they trusted and trained someone else to operate the control station at Unit C, that he would move her out. This incident made him want to move her out of Emerald City even more. In fact, the only thing he loved more than her was his squad, and in his heart, he knew that one day he would have to choose between the two.

When the truck pulled up in front of Unit C, the women felt a sigh of relief. It had been just twenty minutes since Carissa told them what happened, and already their men were there and on the job. The sparkling black truck and spinning chrome wheels represented safety and a peace of mind to them.

One by one, they all hopped out of the truck, to reassure their women, that they had everything under control. Just their presence alone, made them feel better.

"How you doin' baby? They touch you? They ain't put their fuckin' hands on you did they?!" Lavelle asked.

"No baby! They ain't get me, but I was so scared," Carissa cried in his arms.

Lavelle and Carissa looked so good together, that they could be brother and sister easily. His Hawaiian colored skin, matched hers perfectly. And right there on Unit C, they held and kissed each other as if it could've been been the last time they saw each other.

"You okay Yvette?" Thick asked, his large and tall body covering hers like a warm blanket.

"I'm fine daddy. I know you gonna handle them niggas so I ain't even worried 'bout it." She tried to convince her man she wasn't punking out or nervous at the turn of events. "Just come back to me in one piece."

"No doubt baby! I ain't lettin' *nothin'* keep me away from this ass," he said pulling her closer to him.

"I want you to go in the house, Mercedes. We gonna have Derrick and them look over the control station for the rest of the night. We gonna handle them niggas believe that,"

Cameron said as he covered her lips with his. "We puttin' shit down tonight so muthafuckas know we ain't playin out here!"

But in all the excitement, all Mercedes could do was cry.

"Come here baby," Dyson said as he grabbed Kenyetta. "Shit is all good so don't even worry 'bout it. Keep my side of the bed warm, cuz I'm comin' home tonight."

In five minutes, the Emerald City squad had managed to eliminate all their fears. But just as quickly as they came, within' minutes they were gone. Gone to handle who tried to take from them, what they worked so hard to build.

One by one the men covered in thick North Face, Sean John and Eddie Bauer coats, ran toward the truck with their heat tucked closely against their bodies. Each of them vowed to put as many bodies on their pieces as necessary. Strapped up and mad as hell, they drove to Unit A as each of them were ready for war.

CHAPTER 6
THE RIGHT PLACE AT THE WRONG TIME
DECEMBER, SATURDAY, 1:18 A.M.

EMERALD CITY

The heroin was coursing through Critter's veins as he sat hidden against the washing machine in Unit A, on the cold dirty floor. Roaches, ants and other bugs ran all around him as he injected the heroin in his body. Although he never felt the original feeling he felt when he first shot dope, everyone knew that Emerald City had the purest shit in the D.C. area.

With his head against the dusty wall, he let the euphoric feeling take over his body. He could have easily spent the rest of the night in the same position, until he saw the lights come on in the laundry room, and heard several voices. Recognizing CJ and Charles' voice, he froze and stayed quietly in his position.

"They fuckin' here man! I'm tellin' you they know something!" Charles, one of Doctanian's runners whispered loudly.

"What the fuck you talkin' 'bout, Charles? For all we know, they could be here lookin' for just *somebody,* and not necessarily us. So stop trippin' and shit! You makin' us look hot," CJ said. CJ was also a member of Doctanian's team.

"Well we have to be cool but careful too. You think Doctanian know something?" Charles asked.

"Naw, but if we start runnin' and shit, they gonna know something's up. If they even think we had somethin' to do with it, they'll kill us," CJ said.

"I hope you ain't playin young. Cuz I can't go out like this. You said it was gonna be easy. You said your girl saw them runnin' out the stash house earlier, and that the shit was in there," Charles said, clearly more upset and nervous than the others.

"I know what the fuck I said. Just chill out and stop trippin'. Let's get back out there for they really start expectin' somethin'," CJ said.

They were almost out the door when they heard movement in the corner. Slowly and carefully, they pulled out their weapons and moved toward the sound. They saw Critter laid up against the wall, with the dirty shoe string still wrapped around his arm, that just moments earlier was used to find his vein. But Critter didn't move. Like a possum in the woods trying to avoid his attacker, he remained still. He hoped they would think he was so doped out, that he didn't hear anything.

"You up nigga!" Charles asked holding the gun nervously in Critter's direction. He was so scared that he would've pulled the trigger the moment he exhibited consciousness.

"That nigga not up! He a dope head that just got high! Dirty muthafucka," CJ added.

"I say we kill his ass anyway. We was talkin' a lot of shit in here just now. What if it gets back to them Emerald City niggas?" Charles asked, ready to be the one to do the job.

Hearing this Critter was so scared that he was almost taken out of his high. Still, he remained in the same state they saw him in. *Dear God please don't let me die like this. Please don't let them kill me.* He thought. Just like so many other people, he found religion *only* when his life depended on it.

"Do it then. I'm outta here," CJ said, as Erick, who was also there looked on. Before leaving Charles alone, Erick took one last look at Critter.

Charles was just about to pull the trigger, when Doctanian, their lieutenant approached them.

"Where the fuck you niggas been? The Emerald City squad is here. Somebody tried to rob Carissa, and they askin' questions. Meet us in the alley 'round back."

With that one statement, Charles was gone. But Critter didn't move until he was sure they were out of sight. And as soon as they were, he picked his self up off the floor. He knew the first thing he had to do was tell the girls what he heard.

Critter was far from stupid. He knew the more they trusted him, the more they looked out for him. This is why the other fiends played him so close. He was the one person they could always count on, to have access to dope at all times. When he felt the coast was clear, he ran out the laundry room, and toward Unit C.

CHAPTER 7

THE BASEMENT APARTMENT
DECEMBER, SATURDAY, 2:17 A.M.

DUCK DOWN

"Donald please stop being nosey! What if they see you?" Latonya asked her boyfriend while sitting on the floor under her living room window.

"We got the lights out! They can't see shit, but shut up before they hear you."

Latonya and her boyfriend were listening to the Emerald City squad reprimand six of their soldiers and their lieutenant from unit A about what happened to Carissa. The members were so close to the window, that with the lights out, they could clearly see the labels on their jeans.

"Now what the fuck happened tonight?" Thick yelled as he walked back and forth looking each of his soldiers in the eye.

Although no new chief had been named after Dex was killed, it was agreed that he would question the soldiers, since his large size automatically provoked fear.

CJ, the youngest soldier on Doctanian's team spoke. "I...uh...don't know, Thick. I'm tellin' you, we were out here all night and didn't see anybody runnin' out or following Carissa."

"Well in order for them to know where she was goin',"

somebody had to know she was there. Now she came through the fuckin' front door!" Thick continued as he stopped in front of CJ. "So what you sayin' now sounds like bullshit!"

His plan was working. He had the young workers shook. He felt it was just a matter of time, before one of them sold the other out. He wanted to let them know that something *was definitely,* going to happen tonight. With Dex being gone, they couldn't take the risk of letting this grave disrespect slide or having it happen again. After all, they answered to Dreyfus, and all he cared about was his money and what happened tonight could have fucked with that.

Meanwhile Lavelle waited eagerly for the opportunity to bust a cap in whoever was responsible for terrorizing the love of his life. And right by Lavelle's side, with their hands tucked in their coats, were Cameron and Dyson waiting for the results.

When Lavelle's phone rang, he started to ignore it. To him there wasn't anything more important than finding out who tried to rob them, and hurt his future wife. But when he saw it was Carissa on the other line, he excused himself from the line up to answer the call.

Under the only light in the alley, his expression turned from that of business to that of rage. His friends noticed the change and immediately knew something was going on. After receiving his information, and ending the call, he slowly walked over to Thick and whispered in his ear.

CJ, Charles and Erick were on edge, as they realized that it was possible that someone fingered them.

The smell of piss and the rats running back and forth only heightened the feeling of dismay and death. Tonight someone was definitely going to die; it was just a matter of who.

"Somethin' definitely getting ready to happen now baby," Donald whispered. "These thugs getting ready to kill somebody, I just know it!"

"I wish you shut the fuck up before they hear you! If you can hear everything they sayin', how you know they can't hear us?" Latonya asked.

"Girl I know these kinda niggas! Didn't I tell you I use to run Benning road with thirty muthafuckas on my payroll? These muthafuckas ain't thinkin' about nothin' but handlin' business. They ain't worried about nobody in a window."

"You don't know them. Niggas today kill people for any reason. I think you should just leave stuff alone," she pleaded.

Donald heard her words, but ignored all of them. The possibility of violence erupting before his eyes excited him. That was one of the main reasons he liked young girls, who lived in the projects. It allowed him to relive his past, and be around all the things he was familiar with. He used to sling coke and heroin when he was a teenager himself. He was in the game all the way into his late 30's, until he started using coke instead.

After he fell off, he lost everything, including his wife, their $500,000 home in Upper Marlboro, and his kids. He broke all the promises he made to her, especially the one of opening a business, instead of selling coke. However, he couldn't stop nor did he want to. He loved the power, the respect and the women to much to settle down. Being this close to danger, only reminded him of what he had while wishing he were still a part of it.

Thick voice was serious. "Doctanian, I'm gonna ask you one more time nigga! So you betta think before you open your fuckin' mouth. Did you have an eye on all of your soldiers at all times?"

"Uh…..yeah….but… at one point I asked CJ and Charles to get me somethin' to eat. I was hungry from pulling all those hours. You know how it is when those testers come out man. But otha' then that, I had an eye on them the entire time. I swear, Thick. I ain't lyin' to you," Doctanian said, praying that someone didn't include him in whatever happened to Carissa.

He was guilty for being a bad lieutenant, but he was loyal and hardworking and Thick and them knew it. Doctanian knew that the lieutenants of Emerald City didn't have the same privilege as the captains of the Emerald City Squad or the ladies of the Control station at Unit C. They had to be out-side, working hand and hand with their crew, only taking brief breaks in between. They were compensated more, but since most of them didn't like serving hand to hand, the extra money didn't give them any real power.

Directly in front of Latonya's window, Jake, the soldier next to the youngest, heard movement in the apartment behind him. He made a mental note to say something when the moment was right. He wouldn't dare say anything now, and risk whatever they had in store for someone else, being given to him instead.

"You were hungry?" Thick laughed sarcastically. "You're in charge of a shop, which earns you more money than the president of the United States, and you were fuckin hungry? Are you serious?"

"Let me remind you muthafuckas of the Emerald City motto: Honor, Loyalty, Obedience and Silence. That's the muthafuckin' creed we live by. Now I understand that self-preservation is the biggest instinct of any man, but in Emerald City, there's no room for that shit!" He yelled as all six of Doctanian's soldiers stood in fear wondering what would happen next.

"Let this be a lesson to all of you. Emerald City not goin' for bullshit. Don't sleep. Dex gettin' killed only made us stronger than ever!" Thick emphasized as the members of the Emerald City squad began to get hype over what he was about to do. Murder.

Without saying another word, he walked up to CJ, and said, "You broke the code. Good night nigga!" *Bang*!

The shot from his nickel-plated 9mm entered CJ's head. The others were disoriented for a moment, but quickly stood back in line as they glanced at one of their members, lying motionless on the ground.

Charles and Erick were petrified. They definitely knew that the possibility was greater now that someone had seen them too. But Erick didn't intend to go out like that. He was ready and willing to bust right back at Thick and anybody else who wanted to kill him, before he just stood still and accepted his fate.

"You can take the next one. He's all yours," Thick said as he looked at Lavelle and faded backwards.

Lavelle stepped up from the position he took at the start of the meeting. His movement was so fluid it appeared he walked on air. Without saying a word, he squeezed two into Charles' face. When Charles dropped, and only when he dropped, did he resume his position alongside his squad. He was glad Thick hadn't forgotten that he wanted a piece of whoever tried to kill his girl. Like always, he remembered, and gave Lavelle the pleasure he needed. Seeing him drop was so satisfying, that immediately his dick got hard.

"I'm not going out like no sucker. Fuck that shit!" Erick thought. With his hands behind his back, like they demanded from all of them earlier, he placed his hand in a position, which would give him quick access to his 9mm. In his mind, his destiny was already chosen and he was willing to accept his fate. But unlike his co-conspirators, he had plans to take at least three of the captains of the Emerald City Squad with

him.

"Now the rest of you niggas get back to work!" Thick said as he saw the only four members left in Doctanian's crew began to leave.

"And Doctanian!" Dyson yelled.

"Yeah?" He said as he turned around nervously.

"Don't worry, these niggas will be replaced."

Doctanian nodded his head, and moved out of the alley and out of sight.

But Erick still couldn't believe he was spared. Whoever gave the message, delivered it incorrectly. There were three of them involved in the plan to rob Unit A's stash house. One thing was for certain, the Emerald City squad wasn't as soft as he thought they'd be after Dex being killed. They were more vicious than ever. He decided to lie back for a while, and resume his plan to rob the stash house later, when he got another crew. And this time he would do it carefully, and leave no witnesses.

When Jake slid back through the door and moved toward the alley, Thick and the others wondered what was up.

"What you doin' l'il nigga? Get back to work!" Dyson yelled. "We got this shit here."

"I am…but uh….I wanted to tell you something," Jake said.

Sensing something was wrong, they listened to what he had to say. After Jake told them of the witnesses that could possibly be behind the window, they realized what they had to do. Slowly and carefully, they directed their attention to the same window, Jake stood in front of earlier. Without hesitation, they each pulled out their weapons, and sprayed the basement floor window full of holes. Not stopping until they emptied all their clips. Latonya and Donald died instantly.

Pleased with how things were handled, they walked off

toward their truck parked on the other end of the alley and into the night.

CHAPTER 8
ON THE STRENGTH OF LOVE
JANUARY, MONDAY, 3:32 P.M.

MERCEDES

"Cameron, you got to talk to your daughter! You know she brought a knife to school last week and almost got expelled."

"Well was somebody tryin' to fuck wit' her or somethin'? Cuz I ain't gonna tell her not to defend herself, Cedes."

"She pulled it out on the teacher, Cameron. That girl is becoming *terrible!* I'm tellin' you, I might have to get some help for her."

"What the fuck you talkin' about get some help for her?! My daughter don't need no fuckin' doctor. So if you thinkin' 'bout that shit, get it the fuck outta your head right now!"

"Well what you want me to do? Keep lettin' her act a fool? I need some fuckin' help!"

Cameron didn't understand that Chante was not innocent anymore. He didn't understand how serious things were with her. It seemed like every time I came in from working the station, my mother would tell me about something else she had done. All Cameron cared about was L'il C. He never put in any real time in with his girls.

"Where's she?" he asked.

"With my mother," I said. "Want me to go get her?"

"Naw. I'll talk to her later. Where's L'il C? I wanna run him to P.G. Plaza tomorrow to get those shoes he wanted."

"He's with her too. L'il C don't need any more shoes. We don't have anywhere to put his shit now." I paused and asked the question I always did when I got my queue. "When we gonna move baby?"

"Stop fuckin' wit' me, Mercedes. We already talked about this shit. Soon as shit is stable, we'll move. Why you keep askin' me when you know how tight shit is around here. Niggas just tried to take us down. We can't be moving away."

"But you have been saying the same thing forever, Cameron. With the money we make and what you get from the other shops, we could at least afford a nicer apartment. I'm not saying we have to buy the house I want. I just need more room for all our clothes and stuff. I'm tired of living like this. Emerald City is filthy."

"Filthy? What you talkin' 'bout, Mercedes. You been livin' around here all your life. It ain't like our apartment ain't laid."

"But what happens when we walk out the door? I got to work overtime right now to keep the roaches and rats from otha muthafucka's apartments creeping over here. I want the life you told me we would have when things got better. It seems like all you care about now is business when you come home."

Cameron stood up from the sofa, and walked over to me. I already knew what he was trying to do. Make me forget about what I wanted by making love to me. And although I knew, I still couldn't resist him. His chocolate covered skin and perfectly sculpted body called me. It didn't help that he wasn't wearing nothin' but boxers and the platinum and diamond chain that hung around his neck.

When he finally reached me, he pulled me into him and

placed his lips over mine. The scent of his Black Code cologne by Giorgio Armani, reminded me so much of what I needed from him. Safety, Security and love.

Unlike my friends, I wanted this lifestyle. But living in Emerald City without being able to escape when I wanted to made me feel no better than Critter or any of the other mutha-fuckas we served. I liked being a hustler's woman but I felt I was losing my man. I was supposed to have everything I wanted, including a place free from the fiends and drug addicts, which made us rich. But I didn't.

"Listen baby…Just give me some more time. We need ya'll here cuz wit' people tryin' to take us down, all we got is each otha'. There's nobody ready right now to run EC, Niggas are on serious crud time. They just waitin' for that perfect moment, to catch us slippin'. You see how many times niggas tried to rob us since they tried to get Carissa right? Imagine what would happen if they saw us packin' up and runnin'? I'm sorry baby, but right now is not the time to leave."

"When *will* it be, Cameron? What about our kids? Don't they deserve better too?" I asked desperately trying to hold back my tears.

"Yes they do baby," he said as he reached in for another kiss and removed my shirt. "Ya'll all do. As long as I got blood in my body, you'll have everything you want and everything you need."

I don't even remember how we went from the living room to the bedroom, but Cameron did his best to make me remember why I made him my man. From sucking my toes, to kissing my eyelids, he made love to me as if he needed me as much as I needed him. As I slid down on his large 11-inch dick, I let my body tell him how much I cared for him.

The look in his eyes as he took pleasure from my wet

pussy reminded me who was really in control. Me.

Around and around, up and down I fucked Cameron like a professional. This was the only real time I had his full attention. This was the only time he let his guard down, and gave into me. We didn't stop making love, until we couldn't do as much as lift our heads. And before I knew it, we were fast asleep.

Cameron ending a call awakened me. I didn't move because my gut was telling me that he was gonna leave again. Ever since Carissa had been set up, they stayed with us night and day. They made their presence known in Emerald City. And after they murdered CJ and Charles, niggas knew they weren't playin'. For two whole weeks we had them all to ourselves; and every time his cell phone rang, I prayed that wouldn't change.

"We gotta go downstairs. Get dressed," Cameron said, in a serious tone.

I hustled to get myself together and did a John Wayne. A John Wayne consisted of me washing my face, my ass and brushing my teeth in the sink. I knew that whatever was getting ready to happen required my immediate attention so a bath was out the question.

I watched Cameron tuck his heat to his body and throw on his thick black coat and I grabbed my big beige coat.

Once off the elevators, the first thing I saw was Thick leaning up against the rails outside with arms wrapped around Yvette's waist. I noticed Carissa with her arm wrapped around Lavelle's as he tucked his hands inside his coat pockets. Finally, I noticed Kenyetta and Dyson sitting on the top step of Unit C looking in our direction. I could tell from the looks on their faces that something was going on.

When I pushed open the building's door, I was nervous. I mean, all of my friends were there but lately too much shit was happening. But when I was outside, I saw my favorite car glistening. The one I had been stashing money aside to purchase behind Cameron's back. A candy apple red Mercedes Benz C-Class C55 AMG with a big black ribbon on top of it. I didn't want to get carried away, but by the way everyone was smiling, I couldn't help but pray the car was for me.

"Baby! Is it…Is it really?" I asked him as he smiled at me.

"I don't know, why don't you take these and find out," he responded, handing me a set of Mercedes keys.

As Cameron gave his boys dap, I bolted down the steps towards my new ride. My girls quickly ditched their men and were right behind me running down the steps. It felt like Christmas day. There was no special occasion, and I wondered what I'd done to deserve such a tight ass present. Once I opened the door, I saw a dozen long stem roses, with a note that read:

"Stick with me baby and I'll make all your dreams come true. One day at a time."

Before I could cry, he came down the steps, opened the passenger door, and sat down. I was so overwhelmed I was speechless. Nothing I could say would express how much this gift meant to me.

He closed the door and I closed mine too. I watched my friends circle around my car inspecting it from the outside.

"I know shit gets rough baby, don't think I don't know. But do you know how good it feels, to have a woman by my side who can hold shit down?! I know a lot of niggas who dealin' wit' females who would be scared as shit to do half of the things ya'll do out here. I need *you* to know, I appreciate everything you do Ma. I *will* get you out of these projects, the moment we get shit right. But you valuable right now baby. You more valuable than you realize. We're building a dynasty! With Dex and Stacia killed, we have to watch each otha's backs. Are you wit' me Ma? Can you be that down ass bitch I know you are?"

I was still trying to formulate words, but I knew my heart and my eyes told him exactly what I felt.

"Yes baby. I can be anything you need me to be. I'll lay down my life for you Cameron."

"That's what's up. Wit' that being said, Mercedes Johnson, will you do me the honor of being my wife?" he asked as he pulled out a four-carat princess cut, FLS diamond ring.

"Yes baby! Yes, I will!" I said as I kissed him.

"You made me the happiest man on earth."

"And you made me the happiest woman," I kissed him and he wiped the tear that fell from my eye.

"Well...let me let ya'll do you. I got something in the glove compartment for you and the girls to chill off to celebrate. We'll get into the details of our wedding date when you get back."

"Thank you baby! I love you so much," I said, meaning every word I said.

When he opened the car door, my girls flooded in.

"Girl let me see!" Yvette screamed as she claimed her spot in the front seat.

"Oh shit! Cameron out did them nigga's major girl! Thick better get his game up." She laughed, secretly saying what she *really* felt.

"What you do to Cameron girl?" Kenyetta asked. "I need to take lessons."

"Yeah I wanna know too!" Carissa said.

"Well for starters I take it in the ass," I laughed.

"Fuck you!" Carissa laughed back. "But if it's like this, maybe I should apply extra KY Jelly." We all laughed.

When we opened the glove compartment, I saw three Morning Fresh air fresheners, which were my favorite and a stack of money.

"Got Damn C!" Yvette yelled out the window. "You want two wives?"

"Naw I'm good." He chuckled on the top of Unit C.

"Don't worry baby! I'ma do somethin' bigger and better than this nigga!" Thick laughed with his boys.

"I just want you to come home more," Yvette yelled slightly ruining the mood with her sincerity.

He winked. "I got you ma."

"I love you Cameron!" I said starting my engine.

"I love you more wifey!" His show of affection in front of his boys added to my ego. For that one moment, I couldn't imagine life without him.

As we drove off headed to Tyson's Corner, in Virginia, I realized that I was willing to stand by Cameron even if we were on our way to hell. I needed him, and if he was willing to make me his wife, I knew he needed me. At least I hoped.

CHAPTER 9
LEADERSHIP STRICKEN
JANUARY, MONDAY, 7:15 P.M.

DOCTANIAN

"You know the Lord don't like what you doin' son. You gonna have to answer to somebody sooner or later."

"Yeah I know Ma but right now, I gotta' do what I got to do."

"You ain't got to be in the streets son," his mother said as her butter soft hands gently touched his face. "You don't have to do nothin' you don't wanna' do baby."

Doctanian hated when his mother reminded him of his life in the streets. She had been questioning him repeatedly about what happened to CJ and Charles. He felt she had a strange way of knowing everything. Although he wasn't the culprit, he knew exactly what happened and it had been eating him up ever since.

Mrs. Madelyn Bright was an active member in church and she hated living in Emerald City. With the money she earned from Social Security she couldn't afford to move. She ran an active "War on Drugs" campaign at church, even though she was unable to prevent what was happening in her own home.

"Ma, look around you? All the food that comes in here I buy. We wouldn't have nothin' if I didn't get out in them streets. If it's not me it would be somebody else selling drugs to them people."

"But baby…you got the gift of leadership. You can make anybody do anything you want 'em to do. You ain't nothin' like yo mamma. I didn't have nothin' past a sixth grade education, but you went all the way. Straight A's and all! Instead of leadin' them young men into a life of crime, you could be helpin' them get out."

Doctanian knew what his mother was saying was true, but he was too deep into things now. He had seen too much. How could he turn back now?

Doctanian was twenty years old and had a beautiful golden brown complexion. His 6'2 inch height quickly made him appealing to all the girls in EC, but Doctanian was true to only one. That was his 18-year-old girlfriend Jordan.

Jordan was light skin with beautiful long hair and a distinctive mole on her upper lip. Her body was well developed, and she chose the right clothes to accentuate her thick ass, and curvaceous body. From the moment he laid eyes on her, she had him. Unlike a lot of niggas in the hood, Doctanian had a heart. The moment he let her know he ran for the Emerald City Squad she sealed her position by his side by sexing him in ways he never imagined. Although younger than him, she had way more experience in the sex department. Now that he'd gotten her pregnant, he was even more loyal to her.

"Ma, I ain't nobody's leader. I can't take on that type of responsibility," he said not realizing that by commanding six men every day, he was doing just that.

"I gotta go, Ma. I'll talk to you later." When he saw the sorrow in her eyes he said, "I love you. But I'm nothin' if I don't take care of you." He placed a kiss firmly on her face and walked out the door.

"L'il C. Come here man!" Doctanian yelled, as he continued to watch over his soldiers. After being reprimanded the night of CJ and Charles' murder, he micro-managed their every move.

"What man!" L'il C yelled back, letting off the vibe that his father ran the hood, and he didn't have to answer to anyone.

"Just come here for a second man!" Doctanian yelled back.

L'il C stopped talking to one of Derrick's workers, and made his way to Doctanian. He looked so much like Cameron, that whenever Doctanian saw him, he immediately had respect for him.

"What you want nigga!" L'il C responded with arrogance. He knew the power his father had and he made sure everyone else did as well.

"I wanna know why you keepin' time wit' Trey and them?" Doctanian responded. "Them niggas ain't nothin' but trouble."

"No reason! We just kickin' it. Why you in mine anyway?" he responded as he laced his Timbs, and brushed off the little bit of dirt that snuck up on them.

"I'm in yours cuz it's not cool to be out here right now man. Where your moms at anyway?"

"She wit' my aunts and them. They rollin' 'round in her new ride."

"Word? What she get?"

"A new Mercedes!"

"Oh for real?!" Doctanian responded, really feeling happy

for her.

"Yeah, but I'm bored as shit!" L'il C said.

"Well let's do this. You chill from out here, and I'll see if your pops will let me take you to Dave & Buster's later."

"For real?!" L'il C said as his face lit up.

"For real l'il nigga!"

Without another word, he took off toward his grandmother's house.

Doctanian was happy because he liked the l'il guy and he didn't want to see anything happening to him. He knew that far too much was happening in Emerald City, and it was best that he stayed somewhere safe. When his tour was over, he called Cameron and made sure it was cool, then he scooped up L'il C and they headed to Dave & Buster's in his black Camry. These were the best of times, but the worst of times were sure to come.

CHAPTER 10

SCARED FOR LIFE
JANUARY, MONDAY, 9:15 P.M.

"Girl, I hope you don't mind me hugging your man when we get back!" Kenyetta yelled from the back seat. "He really looked out with the money he gave us today for shopping."

"Yes I do mind you hugging my man!" Mercedes yelled.

Everyone got quiet. I couldn't believe she was acting funny already. Hell, they weren't even married yet and already she was acting territorial.

Mercedes started laughing. "But I don't mind you hugging my *fiancé*."

Everyone laughed.

We were out of the parking lot, and on our way back to DC, when I remembered I left my Tiffany's charm bracelet at the store.

"We gotta go back, Mercedes," I yelled.

"Why what's up?"

"I left my bracelet in that damn shop," I said looking in my empty blue Tiffany box.

"Girl! I knew you were gonna do that shit," Kenyetta said. "That's why I told you to put it back in your box after she finished polishing it for you."

I told her. "Hindsight is twenty-twenty."

When we got back to the Tiffany's parking lot, I tried to hurry inside to get my bracelet before they closed. But the person I saw coming out the door, stopped me in my tracks. I saw the same girl the day of Stacia and Dex's funeral. The same girl Thick consoled as if she belonged to him. The exact same girl I had several nightmares about, ever since I saw her face.

"Oh....Hello, Yvette," she said as if she saw a ghost.

"Hi," I responded surprised she knew my name. "I'm sorry, do I know you?" I added hoping she would provide some info about herself, like who was she, and what her relationship to my man was, especially since it was obvious that she knew so much about me.

"I'm a friend of Stacia and Dex. My name is Zakayla." She smiled as she reached out her hand to me.

"A friend of Stacia and Dex?" There was no way she was a friend because any friend of Stacia's was a friend of mine.

"Yes. I met you at the repast remember?"

Not only was her presence threatening, but she was also a liar. I never formally met this bitch. I took notice to the diamond rings on her fingers. They were huge and I could tell whoever she was, she was definitely being taken care of. What stood out the most was the scar she had on her chin. I couldn't help but feel a little jealous, that she and Thick shared a similar flaw.

"Oh...yeah," I smiled slightly. "Well....Hello, Zakayla," I said trying to pull myself away from noticing how beautiful she was. "It was nice to meet you again, but I really have to go now, my boyfriend is waiting on me to get back home," I lied. "Maybe I'll see you around."

"Yeah...Maybe," she said as she walked out the door.

When I grabbed my bracelet and rejoined my friends in the car I was out of it. Prior to seeing that bitch, we were having such a good time. I didn't bother telling them. Besides, I didn't want them telling me I was trippin'. Not to mention I wasn't trying to ruin the evening. But all I could think about was whether there was something going on between her and my man that I needed to know about.

Unfortunately, the answer had just stared me right in the face but I wasn't tryin' to see it.

CHAPTER 11

WHAT ABOUT ME
JANUARY, THURSDAY, 9:22 A.M.

KENYETTA

"That's tight that they're getting married. You think we could ever make a move like that?"

"Baby, stop tryin' to follow behind everybody else. The only reason Cameron is marrying that girl is 'cuz they got like twenty kids together." He laughed as I helped him pack his clothes to leave me for the weekend.

He and the other captains of EC squad were going away to look after the other shops. They had spent so much time at Emerald City that the other places were starting to suffer. We weren't as mad as we thought we'd be because we never expected them to stay so long to begin with. On a regular out of a week they came home three days.

"I'm not following behind anybody baby. It's just that I know we haven't been together forever, but I still want a commitment Dyson.

"Listen," he said as he threw his packed bag next to the door. "I can't be pushed into doin' nothin'. When I put a ring on your finger you're gonna know I'm ready and it won't be four carats like Cam gave Cedes. It'll be a carat for every year we been together."

Looking at Dyson's muscular body made me want him all

over again but what he said about not wanting to marry me got in the way of how I wanted to express that.

"What's wrong with my little Indian girl?" he asked as he pulled me to him. "Did I tell you how sexy you look today? My man was tellin' me the otha' day how these niggas be tryin to get at you and Carissa. Don't let nobody come near my pussy!" he said.

I thought that comment was ridiculous. Why would I want the jesters when I had a king?

"I won't baby," I said, smoothing my hair back with my hands. "Call me later."

When he walked out the door, I looked through the mail and sat in the living room with my grandmother. She was far too nosey and lately I'd been doing everything within my power to avoid her.

"Hey, Granny. How you feelin'?" I asked courteously.

"Oh now that your little boyfriend is gone, you wanna stop neglectin' your grandmother. Well don't waste your time! If you ain't spend no time with me then, don't worry 'bout me now."

"Granny, what are you talkin' about?" I asked not really wanting to know.

"I'm talkin' about you sending me away for the past few weeks so you can be a whore!" she yelled pointing her wrinkled finger in my direction. "And what's this I'm hearin' about Mercedes marrying that Cameron boy?!" Without waiting for an answer she continued, "All ya'll ain't nothin' but a bunch of criminals terrorizing what use to be a nice neighborhood."

"Bye, Granny," I said realizing even more why I shipped her off whenever I got a chance.

I walked in my bedroom and lay across my bed. My mind went through all the events that happened over the past few weeks, including Cameron's marriage proposal. Maybe Cameron and Mercedes would be the next Stacia and Dex.

I missed Dex so much. He was there when I needed him the most a little over a year ago and it's only because of him that I'm even still living. I don't know what I would've done if he hadn't shown up the night he did.

Dyson had just left out of the house, after threatening to end the relationship again. He had done that from time to time, whenever he wanted an excuse to see other women. My grandmother was gone on an overnight convention at church. Dex had come up to see Dyson regarding a new shop opening up in Oxon Hill, Maryland but he had just missed him. When he noticed my front door open, he walked in.

"Kenyetta what are you doin'?" Dex asked me, as I sat on my apartment floor with a gun in my hand, preparing to take my life.

"Nothin'!" I sobbed. "Why are you here anyway, Dex?! Your friend broke up with me and left again! I hate my life!"

"Don't say that shit!" he said staring at me with concern. His eyes fixed on the weapon.

"It's true! Why can't I make him happy?" I asked as I began to cry harder.

"Kenyetta," he said as he took the gun out of my hands, carefully. "That dude may have a lot of shit goin' on but one thing's for sure, he loves you."

"How do you know? All ya'll are probably the same anyway," I said as he helped me off the floor and to my bedroom.

"What you talkin' about girl?" he said flashing the smile I was sure won Stacia over.

"I'm talkin' about if a girl is not a supermodel type ya'll don't want to be bothered."

"Have you seen yourself, Kenyetta?" he asked as he sat on the chair next to my bed.

"Yes... And?" I said, not feeling up for bullshit.

"And you're fuckin' beautiful! I'm tellin' you right now, if I wasn't fuckin' wit' Stacia, you woulda been my girl a long time ago."

When I lifted up off the bed to look into his eyes I noticed they had changed from when he first came through my door. For the first time ever I could tell that Dex, the one man every woman lusted after, wanted me.

"But why? What's so good about me?" I asked hoping he could convince me that I was worthy of anybody, let alone him.

"Well, I'm a sucker for that soft hair and chocolate skin. It's not often you see a beautiful woman with both. Plus, that ass, I'm tellin' you shawty. Dyson has caught me a few times checkin' you out. You a dime, Kenyetta, it's simple as that. I don't know what's goin' on with you and Dyson, but he'd be a fool not to want you."

I was beginning to feel better. Dex thought I was attractive but I figured he had to be lying about wanting to sleep with me. He had to be saying all of that, just to prevent me from pulling the trigger. But I could tell he was willing to go as far as he had to, to save my life.

Lie or not, I felt better about myself and it was all because of Dex, but now there was another problem. I wanted him. I wanted him in my bed and I wanted to feel him inside of me. I know it was wrong for having these feelings. Stacia was one of my best friends in the world. But I needed him...just for one night, I wanted to know how it would feel to be with the chief of Emerald City. Above all, I needed to *feel* loved.

My wish was granted when he moved toward the bed and gently kissed me on my lips. His kiss was gentle but passionate, something I'd never gotten from Dyson before. Softly and as if he loved me, he moved his soft lips all over my face while removing my nightgown.

"I'm afraid, Dex."

"Don't be baby. Let me love you for one night. Let me show you how you deserve to feel. Let me show you how shit would be, if you were my lady."

With that declaration, I gave into him. His soft sucks on my breasts made my toes curl. When I thought I couldn't take it anymore, he methodically ate my pussy, as if he'd been dreaming of it. For the first time ever, I reached an orgasm through oral sex, and I had Dex to thank.

But what we did next, we would forever be wrong for. He removed himself from his jeans and without protection, entered my body, which was anxiously waiting on him. That night Dex made love to me, and it was the first time I'd ever made love. He held me until 6:00 in the morning and in more ways than one, he saved my life.

We never talked about it again, knowing what we shared would always be kept between him and me.

To this day, I'd always love Dex for what he did for me. And I'll never know if he thought about me as much as I did him.

CHAPTER 12

JUST ANOTHER DAY
JANUARY, SUNDAY, 6:22 P.M.

THICK

Thick was running shit around the Southside of DC.

The shops he started in the areas surrounding Emerald City were quickly making him one of the richest dealers in the area. Thick had another purpose that he wouldn't stop at until it was complete. That was taking over Emerald City and securing his position as the new chief.

"Why you taking me home now Thick?" Zakayla asked while his Ford Excursion truck made its way toward home.

"Look, you know what the deal is. I got shit to take care of back in the city. I'll get up wit' you later baby! Why you trippin'?"

"You sure you not trying to get back to Yvette? I mean, when you gonna tell her about us, Thick? I can't keep livin' like this. Either you gonna be with me, and work on the family we supposed to have, or you gotta leave me the fuck alone."

Thick hated how women claimed they could handle a man with a double life, and the moment they got feelings, would start pressuring niggas and shit.

"Look, don't start pressuring me, Zakayla! I don't need this fuckin' shit. I got enough to deal wit' at home wit'

Yvette," he yelled in a tone so loud, it rocked his truck the same way his speakers could.

"Who the fuck you talkin' to, Thick? If it's gotta be like that, don't worry about comin' back to me. Shit, I need a man full time."

Thick couldn't push Zakayla's emotional buttons the way he could Yvette's. He knew that although she loved him, she would've wasted no time cutting his ass off. She already had her ex-boyfriend sneaking around, just waiting for his ballin' ass to fuck up. Zakayla dumped Irvin because he was too weak, and unlike Thick, he didn't know how to handle a woman with her own mind.

He pulled over at a park along Route 40, in Ellicott City Maryland, a few minutes from the apartment that he put Zakayla up in.

"Listen, I'm feelin' you and I know you know that shit, but I'm a man baby, and a man can't be given too many ultimatums. All you gonna do is push me away. Now you know good and fuckin' well I wanna be wit' you. So stop lunchin' out, when you know I got shit to take care of."

She turned around and faced him. Immediately causing him to became humble the moment he looked at her beautiful face, when just moments before he was narcissistic and full of himself. Everything about Zakayla was beautiful. Her dark complexion and thick long eyelashes gave her an angelic look. Just looking at her, you would never expect that she was the future wife of a hustler. Thick had planned to marry her sometime next year.

"Okay baby," she said playing on the fact that her beauty mesmerized him. "Why don't you put your seat back, Daddy. I wanna give you a l'il somethin' to remember me by while you're on the road back to DC."

Obedient and horny, Thick did exactly what he was told.

Zakayla moved her body over his, which was a petite, size 4 waist, phat ass and 36-D titties.

Gently she pulled his dick out of his jeans, and placed him raw, inside her wet and eager pussy. She wasn't fucking him, she was fucking the power he represented. The life she wanted. She covered his mouth with hers and rotated her hips until he came. Thick thought Zakayla *was* on the pill, so cumming inside her was a privilege that she offered that Yvette couldn't. If they didn't use a condom, Yvette made sure he pulled out and he hated it.

When Zakayla was done, she sat silently in her seat on the ride home. In her mind there was nothing else to say. She wanted the last thought he had of her, to be their sexual encounter. Examining her engagement ring, she felt even more confident that he would go through with everything he'd promised.

Since the day he proposed to her, in front of the Emerald City squad and her friends, she had been planning their wedding. When they arrived at the apartment, where he paid the rent, he walked her to her door to see her in safe. Back in his truck, he tried to prepare himself for dealing with his other life, all the while knowing he was nowhere near ready.

Thick didn't have time to shower before he went home to Yvette. And as most men did sometimes, he underestimated how smart his woman was. He came through the door, and put one arm around Yvette's waist and pulled her to him. Yvette had one thing on her mind, examining her man to see where he had been, before he was able to jump in the shower.

"What you make to eat boo?" Thick asked moving toward their refrigerator.

"Nothin' yet. You want me to make some of them cheddar cheese burgers from Murry's?"

"Yeah, that's cool," he said irritated, that he had to ask her to cook when she knew he was coming home.

That was another way Zakayla won him over. She took care of him, and treated him in a way that all men loved to be treated. In addition, Zakayla worked out regularly, and took good care of her body. Lately, Yvette had been gaining more and more weight, and the size 10 body Thick had grown attracted to had been replaced with a size 14. With all that said, Yvette was still cute and most men around the block loved her thickness just as much as they loved the way she was able to hold Emerald City down. Thick on the other hand, was beginning to hate it.

The other thing that made Thick choose Zakayla instead of Yvette as his wife, was how they survived a car accident together, which scarred both of their faces. Zakayla went to Love nightclub in DC one night, and had seen Thick blessing the bar with his cash by ordering drinks for everybody in VIP. He told her that night that he was visiting his sick cousin, and couldn't chill with her.

She was even more hurt when she saw a few of her so-called friends, taking from the money that was supposed to be in her pockets. They didn't even bother calling her to tell her he was there. What upset her the most, was this girl who appeared to be glued to his arm like the diamond emblazoned Movado watch he rocked. When Zakayla made her presence known, she left the club and Thick quickly followed her, leaving the Emerald City squad behind.

When they finally made it outside Thick ran after Zakayla desperately trying to rearrange in her mind what she'd witnessed.

Walking angrily to her car she made up in her head that she didn't want to hear anything he had to say. As far as she was concerned, he was disrespecting her. What Zakayla didn't count on was Thick overpowering her and throwing her in his truck.

Without asking, he lifted her up off her feet and put her in his Cadillac truck, and locked her in her seat belt. In spite of the fight she put up, she still ended up in his passenger seat on the way down the road.

Drunk, he took off driving afraid that he may have lost the one female that excited him since he first met Yvette. Without looking, he ran into another car, which ricocheted and hit his truck again. Thick was thrown through the truck window, and Zakayla while still wearing her seat belt, received minor concussion and the scar she wore on her face today. Thick didn't mind being scarred up, saying that the marks they wore brought them closer together. Six months later, he asked her to be his wife.

He never told Yvette the full truth; he told her he was in the truck alone the night of the accident. Catering to his every need, Yvette nursed the man that hurt himself confessing his love to another woman, back to health.

"Make love to me now," Yvette demanded, trying to see where his head was.

"Naw….let me jump in the shower first. Them niggas out there had me chasing they asses 'round the block for my cash tonight. I'll hit you off when I'm done though," he said, while moving toward the shower.

"Thick! Stop fuckin' playin' wit' me. Whenever you want me, sweaty, dirty or not, I give it to you. Now I'm tellin' you right now to get the fuck over here."

"Who the fuck you talkin' to yo?!"

"Yo?!" She repeated. "Is that where she lives? In bamified ass Baltimore?" Yvette asked, picking up on the "YO" he used at the end of his sentence.

"Bitch get the fuck out my face and fix my food!" he said as he moved to the bathroom and jumped in the shower.

Frustrated, Yvette quickly picked up the phone, to call her girl.

"Kenyetta. Do me a favor." She asked when she answered.

"No problem. What you need?" she asked willing to do whatever her friend wanted.

"Is L'il C outside?"

"Yeah he out here why?"

"Send him up here to get Thick's car keys. And I want you to run the *Overhaul* on his ass for me."

She knew Yvette knew exactly what the *Overhaul* meant. It meant running through that nigga's truck, until she found any signs of him being with another bitch.

"I'm sending him up now," Kenyetta said hanging up.

Five minutes later, with Thick still in the shower, L'il C came upstairs.

Before she opened up the door, she already had the money for him. L'il C was young but he wasn't stupid. He didn't do anything unless it was something in it for him. Although he had no idea of why he was giving Thick's car keys to Kenyetta, he did know that something was definitely up.

Handing him a crisp $50.00 bill, and reminding him to keep his mouth closed, she sent L'il C back downstairs to complete her mission.

Ten minutes later, Thick got out the shower wrapped in a towel and walked into their room to get dressed. *Black bastard!* She thought to herself. *Yeah, I got your ass now.*

Fifteen minutes later, L'il C returned with the car keys. As he was handing them to Yvette, Thick walked out the room, and toward the door.

"What's up l'il nigga? Where your father at?"

"I don't know young!" he responded in that same arrogant tone.

"Word? Well look, did your father give you them Jordan's I picked up for you?"

"Yeah thanks man! Them joints is tight!"

"No problem l'il nigga. What you doin' up here anyway?" he asked.

Yvette on the other hand was scared to death. If Thick found out she sent somebody on a rampage through his truck, he would fuck her up. It never dawned on her that he might catch L'il C bringing back the keys. She was deadest on her mission and that was the bottom line. But she smiled as she found out that already, L'il C had learned to lie, like most men eventually do after they come out of pampers.

"I came up here for you man! I saw your truck out front and wanted to know if you can give me $50!"

Thick began to laugh because he was amused that L'il C was already about gettin' money. He liked him and liked the way he had turned out.

"I ain't got $50.00 l'il nigga, but you can keep this $100.00."

"That's what's up uncle Thick!" he said as he grabbed the cash and ran out the door.

That was smooth. Yvette thought, smiling with relief. *That boy made $150 in less than twenty minutes.*

When her phone rang, she excused herself from Thick to answer it.

"If it's Carissa and them, tell them you tendin' to your nigga and can't be shootin' the shit wit' them all night. Ya'll can talk later," he said sarcastically.

"Whatever Thick!" Yvette shot back as she moved to the bedroom to take the call privately.

"Bitch you heard me right?!"

"Yeah Thick," she said partially defeated.

"Make it quick!" he stated.

When he was done with his demands she turned her attention back to the call.

"So what's up?!" she whispered anxious to see what she had found.

"He ain't have no condoms or nothing like that."

Disappointment washed over her. "Oh."

"But I did find something else, Yvette."

"What is it!?" she asked as her heart rate sped up.

"His T-shirt was in the back seat, balled up. When I opened it I saw some shit on it that looked like nut or somethin'."

"What?!"

"Yeah girl. Nut. Big "T" is definitely steppin' out on you."

Yvette had heard enough, she knew what kind of man she had and she knew it was nut. He had taken his shirt off plenty of times when they were together sexually in the car or not and he always used it to wipe himself off. What hurt the most was that he had sex in a truck that was in her name. Thick didn't have credit and couldn't even get an apartment in his own name if he wanted to. This was an extreme violation.

"Thanks Kenyetta."

"You need anything?" she said in a concerned tone. "Wanna get some drinks at my place?"

"Naw...I'll talk to you later." When she ended the call she stared at him unnoticed. It angered her that he was all posted up as if nothing happened.

Always a soldier, she went about her day and cooked his meal. She wanted to say something but didn't.

Number one he would fuck her up for violating his pricy, and number two, he'd be mad at Kenyetta for going in hi truck.

She sucked it up, and decided to follow him the next time he wanted to take one of his weekend trips. As tough as she was, the only thing that scared her was losing him. But something told her that, she already did.

CHAPTER 13

LIKE BALLA'S DO
JANUARY, FRIDAY, 9:30 P.M.

THE EMERALD CITY SQUAD

In a hotel conference room tucked away in downtown D.C., members of the Emerald City Squad were dressed in all black. Outside of their distinguishing facial features, all that could be seen in the room were platinum and diamond chains and diamond emblazoned watches. The squad was coming up quickly and at this point in the game they could do anything they wanted financially.

The Emerald City squad didn't cut corners when it came to their meetings. They believed that a man could do his best thinking, when in the company of beautiful women, bomb weed, good drinks and good food. So for entertainment they hired strippers from the former Club 55 and had every color from dark chocolate to French vanilla, to please their eyes. Fat breasts, small waist and round asses, aroused their minds, and their bodies. In the dimly lit room, four strippers wearing nothing but black thongs and black stilettos with steel heels were entertaining them while they held their monthly meeting.

Several issues needed to be addressed regarding Emerald City and their surrounding shops. Although not originally intended, the Emerald City squad was quickly beginning to reign as the most vicious crew in D.C. Niggas knew from all around that if you messed with one of the shops EC ran you would have to deal with the entire crew instead of just one of them.

"So what up wit' this Derrick thing? I hear that nigga's causing problems around Emerald City," Dyson said.

"What you mean what's up wit' him? That nigga gettin' paper, so we all gettin' paper," Thick said sipping Hennessey and Coke, while rubbing his hand up the thigh of one of the baddest strippers in Washington D.C.

"That nigga may be getting paper for now," said Cameron who was already tired of the shit he was giving his fiancé. "But if he can't respect the girls, he gonna have to get paper somewhere else!"

Thick pushed the stripper to the side. "Oh, so you makin' the rules now?"

"I'm not makin' the rules man, but I am making sure that this issue gets some real fuckin' attention. Mercedes ain't blowin' you up every time this nigga feel like he don't wanna follow the rules, she blowin' me up! Now we all know that Mercedes is in charge of collection, and since she gotta deal wit' dude all the time, we need to put his ass in check!" he said, as he sipped Belvedere from his cup.

The meetings used to be ran by Dex, but after he was murdered, they decided to keep them going, with a new person running it each month. That person would be in charge of the strippers, food, and the location. They never held their meetings in the same location, leaving nothing to chance. They knew that the more predictable you were, the more you increased your chances of being caught slippin'. And with the heat they brought around the hood, they had made plenty of enemies.

Lavelle yelled, "Okay everybody calm down. We need to

weigh everything before we make a decision about Derrick!" He took a draw of his weed. "What exactly are the girls sayin' he's doin' Cam?"

"You know how women are—"

Before Cameron could finish speaking Thick interrupted him. "Yeah I know how they are. And that's what the fuck I'm talkin' about. Anytime you got bitches runnin' shit, niggas is gonna be mad emotional. It's natural. Shit, I don't want to hear half of the shit Zakayla be givin' me. It's in a man's nature to give a bitch orders, not take orders from 'em. Derrick just probably use to us runnin' shit that's all."

Cameron added, "Well shit has changed, Thick! The girls are holdin' down that operation for us."

"Ain't nothing changed man. They still moody bitches. I'm sure if you talked to Derrick, he'd have something else to say about it. We shouldn't be comin' down on him on bullshit. That nigga's station stays pumpin'! Everybody gotta give."

"Yeah but if we think like that, all we doin' is givin' niggas a free past to fuck wit' them, which is fuckin' wit' our money," Lavelle insisted. "We got to keep nigga's in check. Fuckin' wit' the girls, should have the same repercussions as fuckin' wit' us would. NO FUCKIN' EXCEPTIONS!"

The squad fell silent. They knew what Lavelle was saying was right. Lavelle broke through the darkness in the dimly let room, by pulling from his weed. The smoke rising from it appeared to break the silence.

"He's right," Thick said, although he hated to be made a fool of over something that now seemed so obvious. Allowing niggas to disrespect the girls, just because they were girls, could fuck wit' their business. He realized more than ever, that no type of disrespect could be tolerated, simply because a nigga was salty. "I'll talk to Derrick."

"Naw man. I think I should do it. You already held the meeting with Doctanian's crew. Lettin' you go again would seem like you're the only one they need to be worried about," Dyson said as he sipped on his drink and pulled a stripper on his lap. "I'll go instead."

Although Kenyetta had accused Dyson of cheating before, he still wasn't the worse one out of the crew. He'd only fuck a girl to relieve stress. But Thick on the other hand had taken things to another level. Behind his back, they all talked about how he was dirty for making Zakayla wifey instead of the woman who helped build their organization. It wasn't the fucking or the cheating that made them upset, it was the fact that by doing Yvette greasy, he was shitting where he slept. The entire operation was on the line.

"Cool," Thick responded, angry that they had peeped a glimpse of the plan he had, to take over Emerald City. "You can talk to him. But I think we should all be there."

Cameron interrupted. "I don't. He hates confrontation so I think Dyson should go alone. Derrick ain't doin' nothing stupid. He'll be a'ight."

With a simple nod of their heads, they reluctantly reached an agreement.

"Alright. Let's move to the next issue. I think we should meet with the ladies more then we have been," Dyson added.

Thick spoke first allowing the liquor and weed to influence his thinking. "Man you ain't 'bout to control my dick."

"What the fuck you talkin' about, "T"? Ain't nobody talkin' about your dick. What this nigga talking about?" Dyson laughed as he looked toward his friends and they began to laugh. This display of entertainment at Thick's expense angered and embarrassed him.

"Well what you talkin' 'bout then nigga, damn! What you really sayin?"

"I'm sayin' that we should hold meetings with the girls each month. And instead of them givin' us bits and pieces of the status of Emerald City, they can give us everything all at once," Dyson continued.

"I agree. Running Emerald City ain't no joke, and for real they holdin' that shit down better than we did." Lavelle laughed. "We should help them out a little more by showing we got their backs."

"Okay. We'll meet with them before we have our meetings each month. That way if there's an issue with them, we can bring it to the table, and discuss how we want to handle it." Dyson concluded.

Thick was growing irritated that he wasn't coming up with any good ideas. "Is there anything else?" he grumbled. "I'm ready to get my dick sucked by one of these bitches."

"Yeah. Hold fast on that shit. One more thing," Dyson said as he gulped down his drink. "Are there any plans to get the girls out of Emerald City? I think livin' over there is fuckin' wit' them. And we all can agree that it's been about time."

This was the first time the question ever came up in a meeting. Individually they gave the women they claimed to love their own answers on the topic. But here in front of each other they were forced to admit what was really on their minds.

"Why is this even bein' brought up?" Thick's voice boomed. "It ain't the right time for them to leave and we know that shit! We need to continue to feed them bullshit, until we can trust somebody enough to run the control station. There's too much money pouring into Emerald City now to change shit up. One wrong move can fuck up everything. So what you bringin' up right now is bullshit." He continued in an audacious attempt to break down an issue that the rest of them felt was serious.

Thick pissing on Dyson's question made Cameron mad. "Look. I plan on marrying Mercedes. I got my l'il man and my girls over there too. Now I'm not afraid of the hood, but my girl ain't happy there no more. It's easy for us to say that shit should be cool because most of us ain't there but two or three days out of the week. But they livin' over there 24-7. That shit ain't right, I'm tellin' y'all now."

"I'm wit' Cameron. My two l'il girls are over there man. This ain't gonna fly for long. They can run shit off EC the same way we do," Lavelle added.

Thick stood up and walked around the table. His sudden movement caused the strippers to scatter. "What I want to know is who the fuck are we *really* loyal to? We have a fuckin' business to run. It ain't like we took them out of suburbia and moved them into the projects. They were born, raised and bred in them muthafuckas! I say this issue shouldn't even be addressed, until we pump enough fear in that muthafucka, that niggas won't even attempt to fuck wit' us. Until then, this shit is dead." Without waiting for a response, he sat back down and picked up his cup.

From the outside, the Emerald City Squad appeared to be falling apart. But in some of their minds, this tension could make them closer if they came through it. Still, Cameron and Lavelle felt it was easy for Thick to trample all over the issue, because he wasn't feeling Yvette anymore. But for them it was hard, because they had vowed to be true to the ones they were in love with.

On the other hand, they swore loyalty to the crew. But sooner or later, something or somebody was going to have to give.

CHAPTER 14

TOO MUCH MOUTH
JANUARY, TUESDAY, 9:00 A.M.

DERRICK

Derrick was deep into his main girl's pussy.

Her pussy wasn't as tight as he liked it to be, but she knew how to work her muscles so well that it really didn't matter. Even though she was his main girl, it was only because he didn't spend time with anybody else. He was too busy. As Lieutenant of the Emerald City's Unit C squad, his real time was spent banking money, and watching over his soldiers.

After busting all of his nut on Shannon's face, he made her get up and grab him a warm washcloth from the bathroom. He couldn't stand laying in the smell of sex for too long. But he didn't feel like moving either. Shannon returned with the wet washcloth and began gently wiping his dick down. When she was done with him she wiped her mouth, hopped on the bed next to him, and began tracing the outline of his muscles with her index finger.

"So what you doin' today? Can you take me to the movies or somethin'?"

"What I tell you 'bout tryin' to make plans wit' me during the week?"

She stared at him trying to remember.

"Don't," he reminded her.

She jumped up and searched the cold floor for her panties. "Well why not?! It seems like all we do is fuck!"

"What's the problem?" He slid to the floor to do his 100 sit-ups and 100 push-up routine. "Besides, you knew from the rip that's all I could give you."

"Please! Save that bullshit! The moment I start feelin' somebody else, you get an attitude!"

He stopped in mid-sit up. "Is that what you think?" He let out a disgusted sound. "Because I don't give a fuck who you deal wit', just as long as it ain't nobody from 'round here."

She stood over him and put her foot on his chest. "Well I guess you wouldn't be worried. Seein' as though you still checking behind a woman you can never have."

He pushed her foot off. "That's your problem. You running your mouth 'bout shit you don't know about. If your mouth wasn't so quick, maybe I could take you a little more seriously. But no woman on my arm can have a mouth like yours."

"Are you sure about that, Derrick? I mean, you tell me all the time about how Mercedes be kickin' shit to you, yet you still like her." She walked away, searching for her bra and clothes.

Shannon's words made him angry. Not because they were lies, but because he didn't know what he was feeling and he hated the idea of somebody else knowing something he didn't. As far as he knew, Mercedes was just a pretty face, and like most women, she had a mouth. He hated how she bossed him around or tried to play him in front of his crew when their money was to be collected. So while part of him was attracted to her, an equal part of him hated her guts.

He wiped his face with the towel on the dresser, and stood up. "Look, I gotta go out there and get my money. So put your shit on and get out."

"Whatever nigga, I'm leavin' anyway! You are so fuckin' sorry. You know if Cameron finds out you're jocking for his girl, you just might show up missing."

Shannon's mouth set him off. He rushed her and pushed her against the wall with his hand around her neck. Shannon's eyes were so big he thought they might pop out of her head. She clawed at his arms while trying to secure her next breath.

"Now what you got to say bitch?!" Her face began to turn red. "Like I said, your mouth is the main reason I will never fuck with you on a serious tip. Now get your shit and get the fuck outta here!"

When he released her, she brushed her soft wavy hair out of her face and headed to the bathroom to put the rest of her clothes on. She couldn't wrap her mind around why she even continued to fuck with him. But when she put on her one-carat diamond earrings and diamond tennis bracelet she was quickly reminded. Derrick spent money on her, and good money at that. He wasn't buying a relationship, he was buying her time. As long as he gave her money, he expected her to be accessible to him any time he wanted her with no questions asked. But lately she was trying to be more like a wife, instead of the paid prostitute she really was.

In the kitchen, Derrick drank some orange juice and ate an apple. His body was his temple and he didn't put anything in it, unless it was pure. No fast food or processed goods went into his body. Although he smoked weed, he'd combat anything somebody said about that by saying it was grown naturally. He was a powerhouse inside and out. Books by Malcolm X, Huey Newton and other black activists filled the bookshelf on the wall. He was by far different on the inside, than most people knew. But he preferred it that way, the less they knew about him the better.

When Shannon finished dressing, Derrick approached her

before she left out the door. She hoped that he felt bad for how he treated her, and was going to apologize. She placed it out of her mind after realizing that him apologizing was as far-fetched as him making her his girl.

"Shannon….next time you come around here just tell them bitches what they need to know. Don't bullshit them when you come through them gates. Them girls ain't playin'. It's business."

Trying to bite her tongue, while not trying to piss him off was becoming harder for her to do. Still, she realized she'd gain nothing by making him more upset than he already was.

"I will...But just so you know, Carissa got mad at me and Sharonda because we knew Lavelle. She acted like it was a crime to know him or something."

He took one-step closer to her. "What you talkin' 'bout girl?"

"Well you know he fuckin Sharonda right? Well…we mentioned we knew him, just tryin' to see where her head was at, and she got all bent out of shape." The light from his kitchen bounced off the earrings and the honey brown fur coat that she wore compliments of his money.

"Why the fuck would ya'll do that bamma shit?!" he yelled.

She shrugged her shoulders. "I don't know. She was actin' all high and mighty, and we thought it'd be funny to put her back in her place. We was just fuckin' with her. It wasn't that serious. After we finished playin' her, we told her what she needed to know."

"Shannon, get the fuck out! And don't call me, I'll call you." He opened the door and slammed it behind her.

Bitches! He thought. He didn't understand why she would have Sharonda in the car in the first place. Let alone hint around to her fucking Lavelle. *I swear that bitch gonna make me knock her ass out!*

He decided not to give any more thought to it because the damage was done and there wasn't anything he could do to change it. He just jumped in the shower, and prepared his self for work.

"Walk wit' me for a sec man," Dyson said as he pulled up on Derrick working in the yard.

"What about my soldiers? You know a lot of shit been goin' on around here."

"I know man. Put one of your best on look out and meet me around back near the community center."

Fifteen minutes later, Derrick did what he was told. Eager to find out what was up, he hustled around the back of Unit C to the community center. Noticing Dyson was sitting in his white BMW 750i Derrick jumped in the passenger seat and locked the door. Once in, Dyson handed him a blunt and Derrick pulled on it.

He laughed as he took another pull before passing it. "So what up man? I know you ain't come here to past the bob wit' me."

He nodded in agreement, as he pulled on the weed inside the cherry tasting blunt paper. "Naw I didn't. But it's a hell of an icebreaker ain't it? This shit comes from my Jamaican connect and it moves faster than I can get it in."

"For real? Well why we ain't got none of this over here?" Derrick asked.

"Because Dreyfus supplies everything for EC man. And he wouldn't appreciate nothing but his product movin' over here. Well look nigga, I ain't out here to beat around the bush.

I just figured I'd hit you off wit' a little bit of ganja, before I tell you what I need to tell you."

"And what's that?"

"You need to stop fuckin' wit' Mercedes and them." He reached under his seat and put his .38 in his lap, with the barrel facing Derrick.

Derrick instantly got heated. "So it's like that? You come out here and pull your weapon on me?"

"Naw muthafucka! What it's like is that you gotta stop fuckin' wit' 'em. If you know the money's due, or they need you on somethin' else, you best be handlin' it," Dyson barked.

Derrick tried to calm down. "So ya'll listen to them, without even hearing me out. This some bullshit young."

"Whatever nigga. You knew we'd be out here sooner or later. We let you fuck with them too long. Now I know you gotta a problem with answering to females, but your problem stops here. You take orders from them, the same way you did from us. Comprendè?"

Derrick was mad.

He felt like reaching in his jeans, and stuffing his 9mm in the same mouth Dyson had just pulled on that blunt with. But working in Emerald City was good money, and this type of shit came with the territory.

So instead of shooting off, he listened.

"Now this shit here requires team work. Me and the niggas know you handlin' your soldiers. But we won't have a problem cutting you off, if you can't get with the program. The *full* program."

"I can get wit' it. But I don't agree with how this is goin' down."

"And why you say that?" Dyson handed him the blunt and he refused.

"I think ya'll got shit messed up. I ain't got no problem

answering to anybody that's filling my pockets. You can believe that! What I have a problem wit' is somebody tryin' to carry me in front of my soldiers. Do you know they had one of my workers come and get me while we were on the grind, because Critter say I ain't give him a tester? What kind of bullshit is that?"

"Well was it true?" Dyson asked, pulling on the last of his weed before putting it out.

"I can't remember man." Derrick lied, knowing full well he couldn't stand Critter. "But even if it was true, that's some bullshit to be callin' somebody up on don't you think?"

"Not necessarily. Critter may be a fiend, but he's loyal to Emerald City. That's why we keep him around and the girls realize that. Putting him on gives us an edge on some of these other projects around the way. That nigga know everybody, even the top officials from when he was in office."

"What office?" Derrick asked.

"Government office. Critter use to be a public official in D.C. Everybody knows that shit. Although he fell off like most muthafuckas do in this game, some of his old friends keep in contact just so they can be put on to our dope. Plus it was Critter who told us that Charles and them tried to get Carissa. If it wasn't for him, we would've never known who those muthafuckas was."

So it was Critter's ass who told them. He thought. *I wondered how he found out. It don't matter, they deserved to die for biting the hand that feeds them.*

Derrick took a deep breath and tried to blow out some tension. "It's like this Dyson, tell 'em to ease off of me and I'll ease off of them. I can't run my camp if my soldiers think I'm soft."

"Cool. I'll tell 'em to stop sweatin' you 'bout bullshit but you gotta do your part too."

When they finished, Derrick went back to work with Mercedes on his mind. As far as he was concerned, it was just a matter of time before they dealt with each other.

When they finished, Derrick went back to work with Mercedes on his mind. As far as he was concerned, it was just a matter of time before they dealt with each other.

CHAPTER 15

BUSTED

JANUARY, WEDNESDAY, 10:37 A.M.

YVETTE

I finally broke down and told my friends, everything that was goin' on between Thick and me.

What messed me up was that most of them already seemed to know he was steppin' out on me. They acted like it wasn't even a surprise. Outside of having Kenyetta go check his truck, I hadn't told anybody we were having problems.

We were doing a stakeout and I had already seen enough to run up on him. But knowing Thick, he'd turn it around into something else unless I had proof. So with Mercedes' digital camera, we were trying to get some good pictures of him taking her to Charlie Palmer's Steakhouse in DC, and to the Shakespeare Theater.

Yeah, he was really pulling out all stops for this bitch. But nothing hurt worse than seeing who he was dealing with. It was the same girl from the day of the funeral and Tiffany's. I didn't tell my friends, but I wondered if the rock she had on her finger, was an engagement ring. Please God don't let it be. I wanted to believe that he wouldn't be crazy enough to propose to someone else over me but right now, I wasn't sure of anything.

"They comin' out of the theater right now!" Kenyetta yelled from the back seat of the Grand Prix we rented. I sat next to her slumped down in my seat. I didn't want Thick to see me.

But for real, he was *still* slippin'. Recognizable car or not, he should've known that somebody had been following him for so long.

But there he was, just as sure as it was night, coming out of the theater, in the dark grey slacks and jacket that I paid for. He looked like a million bucks when he cleaned up, and with his body and build, I know she was losing her mind.

"Did he just kiss her?" Mercedes asked as she took pictures of them in the truck. She was in the front with Carissa.

"It looked like it," Carissa said. "Thick has lost his muthafuckin mind. I say we run up on him right now, before they pull off. Fuck da bullshit."

"I'm wit' Carissa, Yvette," Kenyetta added looking at me for approval. "We seen enough. Let's handle this shit now."

They were right, but I didn't want to do it right here. I needed to find out where she lived and where he'd been laying his head every night. So for forty-five minutes we followed them to her apartment in Baltimore. The moment I saw him leaned up against his truck with her in front of him kissing on him I decided to jump out.

My heart dropped as the man I would have done anything for violated me. Here I was his flunky, running an operation that he should've taking care of, and this is how he repaid me, by breaking my fucking heart.

We all got out of the car, but they couldn't keep the pace I was givin'. With his arms wrapped around her, and his tongue in her mouth I snuck up on him from the side of his big ass truck and said, "Is it that good to you? That you would risk everything we have together?!"

He stopped and on instinct pushed her away. She immediately backed up sensing what I was gettin' ready to give. And as mad as I was, I knew she wasn't ready for it either.

"What you doin' here, Yvette?! Who watchin' EC?" he yelled trying to flip the shit and put it back on me.

"Fuck you, Thick! Is this were you've been going? Is this where you've been spending your time? With this bitch?"

I was loud and I didn't care. I wanted to break up the peaceful serenity in the place she lived. Why should she live like a queen and my living conditions be fucked up? Here I was living with fiends, and criminals, and this bitch is over here in B-more living like a princess.

"Who you callin' a bitch?!" she snapped.

I ignored her because I was focused on his bitch ass now, and my girls were already on the job.

"I'm tellin' you right now, if you want your ass whipped, make anotha muthafuckin move!" Carissa said with her hand in her purse.

Yeah bitch! I thought. *This is how we do it! Southside style baby!* She was so shook, she didn't move.

"Answer the question, Thick! Is it worth it? I see you livin' it up out here, and got me living in trash. Why, Thick? Why you doin' this to me?"

"You livin' in trash? Are you serious?! You wouldn't be living in trash if you'd clean your fuckin house you nasty bitch! Half of the time I ain't home because it's too muthafuckin dirty! I'm tired of that shit, Yvette!"

The embarrassment I felt overwhelmed me.

I felt like I did the best I could do. He wanted me outside fourteen hours a day, and he wanted me to be his wife, mother and friend. I didn't have time to clean my house and I barely had time for myself.

"So now you tryin' to play me in front of your bitch and

my friends? If you had a problem wit' somethin' why you ain't tell me, Thick? You are dead wrong right now and you're actin' like I'm the one to blame. Why baby? Don't you love me?"

He was silent and I was hurt. Here we were, outside in front of the friends I considered family and the love of my life acted like he could care less about me. The only comfort I had right now were my girls. I knew all I had to do was say the word, and they'd stomp his pretty girlfriend out. I wonder how much he'd like her then.

"Let me ask you somethin' Thick, and be real wit' me. Are you gonna marry this bitch?!" I asked him not really prepared for the answer. "I see the ring on her finger, and since you ain't bother to put one on mine, I wanna' know."

The bitch called from the sideline, "Tell her the truth, Thick. Let's get this over with."

"Listen bitch! Mind your muthafuckin business before I kick your fuckin ass!" I yelled. I was tired of her mouth. I hadn't addressed her yet because I believed in dealing with the man. But since she insisted to get in the business, she was getting ready to see how I beat bitches down on the block.

"Naw you ain't doin' that," Thick said taking up for her. "You ain't gonna fuckin' touch her."

"And why not? She's stealin' my man *and* talkin' shit," I told him as tears rolled down my face.

"You ain't doin' that because she's carrying my baby. Now I'm sorry you found out like this, but tonight I'm celebrating. She givin' me somethin' you never could. A son."

For a few seconds there was nothing but complete silence. I never realized that Baltimore had peaceful places like this. All I could hear were the crickets trying to be heard above the low hum of passing cars. My world was ending. Everything that I fought for and everything that I believed in was vanishing and I didn't understand why.

"Uuggghh, Thick! I didn't even know you were grimy like that!" Mercedes said. "This don't make no damn sense!"

"This between us!" he yelled. "So step the fuck off."

His new girlfriend quickly moved to his side, as he put his arm around her to comfort her.

He used to do that to me. What changed? What fucking changed! I loved him with all my heart and I felt like that wasn't good enough.

My eyes filled with tears blurring my vision. He didn't even bother to console me. He just looked at me as if I was another issue he had to deal with before moving on with his life. The anger I had before diminished. I decided that I had one chance to fight for my man. One last chance. On my knees, outside in front of my friends and the bitch who had stolen my man's heart, I begged.

"Baby.....please don't do this to me," I said as I grabbed his leg. "Please don't leave me like this. I'll be a better woman to you I swear. On my life I promise to be everything you need."

His girlfriend huffing and puffing didn't bother me. I knew I was disgracing myself but I would've felt worse if I didn't at least try.

"You gotta give me a chance baby. I'll lose weight, clean my house better, anything you want I will do. I'm nothing without you Thick. Everything I do don't mean shit unless I have you in my life. Baby please. I'm the one. I'm the one you trust baby. I'm the one that would lay down my life for you. Don't walk out on me, Thick."

I could hear my friends crying behind me. Kenyetta had already walked to the car because it was too much for her. But I felt that nobody understood more than them why I was doing what I was doing. I know those tears were filled with sorrow for me, and the realization that this could be them right now. And I'd put my life on it, that they'd be doing the same thing to.

But my pleas landed on deaf ears. He kicked me off his leg like I was a crack head trying to get a rock. My friends rushed by my side and helped me up. And it's a good thing they did because my legs couldn't move. All I could think about was what I could've possibly done to deserve this.

"It's over, Yvette. You and me are business partners, but this right here is my future wife. Now I'm sorry it gotta go down like this. I really am. But I'm not in love with you no more. I didn't know it was gonna turn out like this. But what we had ends here."

"I'm glad you laughing bitch! Cuz he gonna do the same thing to you too!" Mercedes yelled.

"Fuck you, Mercedes!" he yelled.

"NO fuck *YOU*, you sorry ass muthafucka!" She shot back.

His new girl smiled at me, as she faded in the dark with my life. He held her hand and moved toward the apartment building. He stopped short and turned around.

My heart skipped thinking he was gonna tell me he made a mistake. That maybe we could work on us after all. But what he said next only proved more that he was through with me.

"I hope this don't affect our business relationship. You the hardest working nigga I know. I'll check you later," he said as he walked off into the night.

Heartbroken and humiliated, I sat in the back seat, as my friends drove me home. Wondering to myself how I was ever gonna make it...*alone*.

CHAPTER 16

WISHING THINGS WERE THE WAY THEY USE TO BE
JANUARY, WEDNESDAY, 6:37 P.M.

It had been three weeks since Thick and Yvette split.

My girl had been taking it bad. She wasn't on post any-more and Emerald City was quickly going down with her. Cameron and them made their presence known, but with them still holding down the other shops outside of EC, they weren't around as much. Several of our runners had been robbed and we were startin' to wonder if they weren't a part of everything that was going on.

"Carissa, one of Harold's soldiers is missin' in action. I think we should go see what's up wit' 'em," I told her as I ended the call with Harold and placed the phone under my chair.

"Damn! I hope he ain't tryin to do us greasy," Carissa said while zipping her Baby Phat waist length coat.

"I'll be glad when Yvette get it together. We need her out here!" Kenyetta said.

"You ain't lyin. How long has he been missin' in action?" Carissa asked.

"A week and a half. The thing is this, you know Harold's squad has been hit more than once over the past week. I'm starting to think it's an inside job."

"Well who slackin'?" Carissa asked, sensing how serious things were.

"It's Key. They probably smokin' up our shit right now."

It's easy to spot which soldiers respect their captains when the going gets rough. Nobody on Doctanian's, Derrick's, Bruce or Jones' team got out of line. Just because we were having issues amongst ourselves, didn't mean it was time for everybody else to fall apart. See Doctanian and them were respected captains and had their soldiers in check with the exception of one of them who attempted to get away. And because of it, nobody tried them as much as they did Harold and Ed's teams. We didn't have any problem from any other squad outside of those two.

"Okay. Let's go over to Unit B, and see what's up," Carissa responded.

"I'm right behind you."

The hallway was dark, the lighting poor and thanks to the leak at the other end of the corridor it smelled musty. Before stepping off the elevator, we scanned the floor. We wanted to make sure another situation didn't happen to us like the one that happened to Carissa.

We quickly moved down the hall toward the apartment. Unfortunately, we couldn't see the apartment due to the bend in the hallway. We arrived at the door and heard voices coming from inside. I placed my hand on my heat and Carissa did the same. We never went anywhere without our fire and although we had them, we never had to use them. However, if Yvette didn't come back to work, I knew it would be just a matter of time before that changed.

We knocked firmly on the door three times. There was no answer but the chatter on the inside stopped.

Before we could knock again, the door flew open. The person who opened it stepped behind it, giving us a clear view of the inside. Before going in, I stuck my head around the corner and saw it was Key's older brother Deuce.

"Come on in," he said blowing out smoke.

"Is Key here?" Carissa asked before going any further.

He nodded toward the living room. "Yeah, he ova there."

When we walked in, Carissa went before me, and I fell back a little. I didn't want anybody rushing us behind, so I wanted to make sure we had all angles covered. I hated having my back turned in places I didn't know. There were six dudes in the dirty 1 bedroom apartment. Two of them were sitting in front of the television playing NBA Live '08 on a broken ottoman, two were sitting on the couch, Deuce was standing up, and the other one was at the kitchen table rolling weed.

"That's a nice ring, Mercedes," Deuce said. "You and Cameron must be stackin' mad money."

As hard as it was, I just ignored his dumb ass.

"Where's Key?" I asked, realizing he wasn't in sight or included in the six men I had counted when we stepped in the apartment.

One of the men sitting on the couch said, "He in the room, he'll be out in a second."

The smell of the apartment was sickening. The dingy walls and dirty carpet told the story of endless drinking and smoking sessions. There was a table filled with weed and the insides of Philly Blunt papers covered it throughout. The couch looked like it use to be cream colored, but it was damn near black.

One minute later, Key appeared from a back room visibly high.

"What up? What you need?" he asked as he joined his friends on the couch. "I know you ain't come over here to give me no pussy. I hear Lavelle and them bangin' y'all's backs out." He laughed with the others.

Carissa looked at me. With my hand on my piece, I made sure I kept my eyes on every one of them. My senses were so heightened that even in the dim lighting of the apartment I could tell you which one of them needed to shower and who was wearing Sean John jeans. I was willing to bust some-body's ass just for moving wrong.

"I need to know why you ain't been back to work. What's up wit' that? You ain't in here smokin' our shit are you?" Carissa asked.

He laughed. "Smokin' *your* shit? Naw. I ain't smoke noth-in' that belong to *you*."

"Okay. Well give us your product and money and we'll be gone. And don't bother about comin' back on the block, you cut off!" I jumped in.

"What the fuck you talkin' bout? I don't ansa to yo ass! I ansa to your nigga!"

"Fuck you talkin' 'bout, Key?! You answer to everybody muthafucka! We put the cash in your hand every week. Now you know the muthafuckin' routine, either anty up our money or product or you *will* be dealt with," Carissa added.

She was passing out threats that, with the way things were looking, I was sure we would have to follow through with.

He stood up and moved toward Carissa with hate in his eyes. "Dealt with?! And just how do you plan on dealing wit' me? What you gonna do? Suck my dick?"

Carissa backed away from him and moved toward me pushing both of us towards the front door. All of them stood up and I could see that whatever was getting ready to happen, was gonna be real bad. They outnumbered us, and although we had guns, there was no tellin' what they had on them.

I grabbed Carissa's arm as we scooted closer to the door. I knew that whatever happened at this point would have to be done by the EC squad. I hated Yvette not being with us because although she didn't say it, I knew she had at least two bodies on her gun.

With Carissa behind me, I snatched open the door and bolted toward the elevators. I could hear my heart beatin' in my ears. I couldn't wait to tell Cameron and the rest of them what happened. When I reached the elevator I turned around and my heart sank to my stomach sank because Carissa wasn't behind me.

Without hesitation, I ran back down the hall and started banging on the door with my gun in hand demanding they open it. When the door flung open, I trained my gun on his gully ass. "Where the fuck is my girl nigga?!"

"Hold up. Hold up! What the fuck you doin' yo?" he stammered. "Your girl ain't here man! Now put that shit down before somebody get hurt!"

"What the fuck you mean she ain't here?" I asked desperately trying to stop the tears from forming in my eyes. I didn't want to remind them that I was a woman and afraid.

Without asking, I pushed my way in and ran through all four rooms including the kitchen and bathroom, but still didn't see her. Excessive amounts of sweat caused my hair to cling to my forehead and my clothes to cling to my body. I felt lightheaded; I knew in my heart that they had done something to my friend. There was no way in hell I was burying another friend!

"Where in the fuck is my friend!" I said pressing my 9mm to one of their heads. I didn't care anymore, if they killed my friend one of them were going with her.

"Listen bitch! We let you run through here. If you ain't see her, that mean she ain't in here. Now get the fuck out!" The older man said as he pushed me toward the door, and into the hallway. When the door slammed behind me, I fell to my knees and banged on it harder but they didn't open it.

Afraid that I lost my friend, I ran to the elevator to get help. I reached for my iPhone and my heart dropped. I had left it on the porch! Shit!

The first person I saw when I got off the elevator was Derrick. Seeing the look of terror on my face must've set him off because he ran to my side to help me.

"What's wrong shawty!? Somebody fuckin' wit' you?!"

I tried to tell him everything that happened through tears and trying to catch my breath. The look on his face, although angry, comforted me. I could tell that he would find out what the fuck happened even if it meant taking somebody out.

We got back on the elevator and I took him to the door.

"This Key house! I just left outta of here," he said as he knocked on the door.

Deuce saw him through the peephole, and without hesitation opened it for him.

"Sorry nigga. We thought you were that bitch!" he said. "Come on in man."

Before they could close the door, I pushed my way in and Derrick knocked Deuce out with the back of his gun. I held my gun firmly in the direction of them muthafuckas because I was sure my friend was dead.

"What you doin' Joe?!" he called him by the name most DC natives gave everyone. "Is this bitch lying to you too?!"

Key said as he jumped up.

Derrick cocked his gun and cut the light on revealing how truly dirty and nasty the apartment really was.

"I'ma ask you one time. If you don't tell me what I wanna here, you gonna have four more holes in your face. Now where the fuck is Carissa?"

"I'm telling you the truth! I don't know where that bitch at," Key said, clearly intimidated by Derrick's presence.

"So why the fuck are ya'll all huddled up on the sofa like some fuckin bitches lookin' guilty?!"

His comment caused me to look in that direction. When Carissa and I came to the apartment, they were all spread apart and now all five of them were huddled on the couch like they were in love. That's when I saw my girl's hand behind of one of the back pillows on the sofa. They were using their bodies to conceal the bump in the sofa, which was Carissa.

"Derrick!" I screamed. "She's behind the pillows on the sofa."

"What?!" He moved toward them.

"They're hiding her under the pillows of that nasty ass couch!" I said as tears ran down my face.

All of them immediately looked shook. Derrick moved toward the couch, and knocked one of them in the face with the gun. I knew right then they were some punks who were only willing to talk shit to women. But when a man approached them, they had their heart taken.

Throwing the pillows on the floor, Derrick lifted her limp body. I noticed the blood flowing from her head and instantly filled with rage. They probably snatched her back on the way out the door and covered her mouth. In one motion, I cocked my gun and put two in Key's head. His friends scattered trying desperately to avoid being next.

I was about to pull the trigger again, but Derrick grabbed

me and told me to come on. I didn't care if war was about to staged they violated in a major way.

"We can finish this later." Derrick's voice bought me back to reality as he cradled Carissa in his arms.

We ran down the hallway and I didn't take a breath until we were on the elevators, and I saw Carissa open her eyes.

CHAPTER 17

FINALLY
JANUARY, FRIDAY, 9:15 P.M.

ZAKAYLA

Zakayla was on cloud nine before she went to the doctor's office.

She had everything she wanted including the man who over the past two years, she fought to have. He had given her everything she ever wanted.

She wasn't remorseful at all about how Thick treated Yvette. She believed all the stories he told her about how nasty she was and how she constantly cheated on him. In her mind, they would've broken up eventually. Zakayla truly believed that she was capable of treating him the way that he should've been treated, since Yvette clearly could not.

All her happiness was squashed when the doctor entered the cold exam room and pissed on her dreams.

"I'm sorry, Ms. Taylor, but you're not pregnant. Take this chart and accurately record your cycle so you can tell when you're ovulating. Don't give up."

"Are you sure? Maybe you should check it again." She begged looking the small chart over.

"I'm positive Ms. Taylor," he smiled placing one hand on her shoulder. "But if you monitor your cycle more closely, your chances to conceive will be increased."

In her mind, lying to Thick about being pregnant was the only way she could've convinced him to leave Yvette, and it worked.

"Girl it's negative again," Zakayla told her friend Lacretia while driving home.

"Well you know what you have to do right?" she asked.

"What?!"

"Just keep fuckin' him!" She laughed. "You'll get pregnant girl."

"I know, I know. But he thinks I'm three months pregnant now. The further along he thinks I am, the harder it's gonna be for me to pass another pregnancy off on this one. The times will be too messed up.

"I understand all that, but at least you'll be pregnant. Thick ain't thinkin' about when the baby is born, he just wants to have a baby. But I do wish you hadn't told him it was a boy. Men are so stupid! A woman would've known that it was too early to tell."

"You're right. But the damage is done. And I'm starting to think I can't have kids," she responded, as she pulled in the parking lot of her apartment complex.

"You can have kids girl. You're healthy. Don't even worry about that. Anyway, has he talked to his ex?"

"No….but he said she's been fuckin' up big time. He has her runnin' one of his shops in D.C. But she ain't been comin' to work lately. Ever since he dumped her for me, she's been falling apart."

"His ex-girlfriend sells drugs for him?!" Lacretia yelled through the phone.

"Yes girl. I told you she was a dumb bitch. I wish Thick *would* ask me to do some bullshit like that. I would cut his ass off so quick he wouldn't know what happened."

"Well maybe he was using her all along. Like you said,

she didn't even clean her own apartment." Lacretia laughed. "I'm surprised he stayed that long."

"Right girl!"

Deep in her heart, she knew Thick still cared about her and him leaving her was a chance she was willing to take. Unlike Yvette, she didn't tell him she wasn't ready to have a baby. She paid close attention to everything he said, and made sure she was everything that Yvette wasn't.

"Well let me go. Thick wants me to cook this big as meal for him tonight. Girl my man is so fucking greedy." She laughed. "Good thing that nigga is paid, otherwise he'd eat us outta house and home."

"Well call me back later."

"Okay. I will."

When she ended the call, she grabbed her purse and parked the 2008 Silver Navigator Thick had purchased for her. He said it was a gift for being pregnant with his first baby. When she stepped out of the truck, she dropped her keys on the ground and bent down to pick them up.

She had her back turned when she was grabbed by her hair and drug along the ground toward the nearby woods at the complex. Zakayla fought desperately kicking and screaming the entire way.

"Shut the fuck up bitch before I slice your throat," one of them yelled.

She did what they said, hoping it was just a robbery.

"Take everything." She cried. "You can take my truck, my purse and everything."

"Don't worry. We will be taking exactly what we came for."

She was able to see that there were four of them, but their faces were covered in black ski masks. Repeatedly they kicked her in her face and stomach. The pain took over

Zakayla's entire body as she begged them to stop. Judging by how hard they were kicking her, she could tell that they wanted her dead.

When she thought it couldn't get any worse, one of them slid off her rings, including the engagement ring that Thick had just purchased for her. She slid back and forth in and out of consciousness.

"This is what happens when you fuck wit' a man that don't belong to you!" She heard a female voice say. Although she was face down in the dirt, with the grass partially covering her face, and the blood dripping in her eyes, she could tell by the curves in their bodies that they were all women.

When she saw three of them running toward the light, a few feet over from where they took her, she thought she might survive. That's when the fourth person hit her in the head with a bat, she was knocked unconscious.

When Zakayla came to, she was in a hospital room with flowers and cards surrounding her. When she tried to lift her head, she couldn't move it. Moving her eyes down as far as she could, she saw the tissue from the bandages on her face.

She looked as far as she could to the left, and saw Thick talking to Cameron, Dyson and Lavelle. She smiled a little seeing that her man was right at her side.

When Thick saw her eyes open, they all ran to her side.

He held one of the only parts of her body not covered in a cast. "You need anything?"

"Some ice," she said, barely above a whisper. "What happened? What's wrong with me?"

"I'll let the doctor tell you baby," he said as he moved

toward the door.

When the doctor entered the room, he asked them could he be alone with her for a little while. When everybody was gone, he addressed Zakayla.

Terror consumed her. "What's wrong with me?" She knew that something definitely happened because of her being jumped.

"Zakayla," the doctor started, his tone even but comforting. "I'm Doctor Polanski and you're at Howard County General Hospital Center. It's remarkable that you survived." He smiled. "But you've suffered an extensive amount of damage to your spine. And there's a real possibility that you'll never be able to walk again."

"No. No," she said as tears fell, soaking the bandages on her face.

The look on the doctor's face made matters worse. She could tell that he was far from finished telling her about everything she needed to know.

"What else?" she asked, unsure if she would be able to take it.

"Well, Ms. Taylor, we've brought in the best reconstructive surgeons around."

"For what!" She cried. Her voice faded away as soon as it left her body.

"For your face, Ms. Taylor. For your face. It appears that whoever has done this to you took a blade and sliced your face over fifty times."

Zakayla felt weak, as the doctor appeared to be moving further and further away from her. She felt like she was moving into darkness, and decided to let it consume her.

The more she tried to talk, the more it appeared to be in vain.

Within minutes, she was unconscious.

CHAPTER 18

IM TRYING
JANUARY, SATURDAY, 12:18 P.M.

Today was the first day I felt like going on.

I never realized how much Thick meant to me, until he was gone. I unplugged my phone weeks ago because I couldn't bear to see the calls from everyone but him. If he wasn't calling me, I didn't feel like talking.

The first thing I did was move everything out of my apartment, and into the basement. The only thing I had left, was my mattress and TV's. I didn't want anything in my place that reminded me of Thick or the life I had with him. I decided that today, I was going to get in my car, buy me some new furniture, and start all over. And because I haven't eaten in weeks, I'd lost a lot of weight. So I'd have to buy some new clothes. I didn't realize how much weight I lost until I tried to slide in a pair of old jeans, and they fell off.

When I plugged in my phone, I was afraid to check my messages. I'd been ignoring calls from everybody since Thick dumped me. People got tired of me ignoring my calls and started knockin' on my door but I didn't open it. All I wanted to do was to be alone.

For the first week, I did nothin' but cry. And when I couldn't cry anymore, I thought about killin' myself. The third

111

week I thought about killin' him, but put that idea out of my mind because I loved him too much. I wanted to talk to my friends but I put that out of my mind too. I was too embarrassed because I knew they knew how long I played his fool.

I decided to check my voicemails. And just as I thought, my mailbox was full. The first message I heard was from Cameron, then Lavelle and then Dyson. I erased them all. I'm sure they were wondering why I wasn't takin' care of my responsibilities with Emerald City, but I knew they understood too. And because I wasn't sure how I was gonna handle things yet, I didn't want to listen to their messages. The next voice I heard made me sad all over again, but I listened anyway.

"What's up, Yvette, it's Thick. Now I know we got problems ma, but this ain't got shit to do with our business with Emerald City. I need you to be strong and handle this shit like I know you can. I still love you. One."

"He still loves me?! Yeah right! Fuck him. I ain't doin' shit else for him. He lost his flunky! If I do decide to go back on the block, it'll be for my girls and not him," I said as I erased through the next few messages from my mom and my friends. I was good until I heard the last one from Mercedes crying.

"Yvette....please pick up! It's Mercedes! Girl, I had to do something tonight. They tried to kill Carissa. I'm at the hospital with Derrick and her now. She's gonna be okay. But I'm so scared. We miss you out here girl. Please pull through! I love you."

What the fuck? Here I was wallowing in my own self-pity and my girl ended up in the hospital. I jumped in the shower, only because I had to. After spending three weeks in the house alone, I wouldn't have been any good to anybody smelling the way I did. I threw on some brand new cotton men's Gap sweatpants, a sweatshirt, and my Timberlands. Then I grabbed my .38 and my black North face coat. I was on my way out the door, when I saw all three of my friends getting off the elevator. It had only been three weeks since I'd seen them but it felt like ages. The moment they saw me, tears filled their eyes and mine too. We embraced each other before we walked into my bare apartment.

"Damn girl," Kenyetta said. "You got rid of all your shit!"

"It looks like a brand new apartment in here. All we gotta do now is paint," Mercedes said."

I didn't say anything. I just stared at the scar on Carissa's pretty face. I felt like shit for letting my girl down. She must've seen the hurt in my eyes.

"It's not your fault. It could've happened to any one of us," Carissa said. Even after she'd gone through something so traumatic she was still trying to console me. I knew we were tougher than a lot of dudes and Carissa just proved it.

"Yeah but it didn't happen to one of us. It happened to you. I'm so sorry, Rissa," I said as I hugged her tight.

I removed my coat and tossed it on the floor.

"Damn girl! I thought I was lunchin' when I first saw your little pea head, but now I'm sure. You did lose a rack of weight," Carissa said.

"I was thinkin' the same thing," Mercedes said giving me the once over.

"So how much weight have you lost anyway? You look good!" Kenyetta asked.

"She does!" Mercedes added. "She tryin to hide that bangin' ass body in that big ass coat."

"I don't know. I haven't weighed myself, but I'm sure about twenty-five pounds."

"Yeah. I bet Thick would be all on that now," Kenyetta added.

When she said that the laughter stopped. Just the mentioning of his name fucked the entire mood up and made my heart skip two beats. I realized even more how much I missed him and still loved him. I guess it was too early, even after three weeks, to be fully over somebody.

"I'm sorry girl. I hit a bob before coming up here so I'm still sayin' stupid shit," Kenyetta apologized.

"Don't worry 'bout it," I said. "I'll get over his fat ass sooner or later."

"Well....we got a treat for you," Mercedes said as they looked at one another and smiled devilishly.

"Well are ya'll gonna stand there lookin' stupid and shit or are you gonna tell me what's up?"

Just then, Mercedes walked up to me and told me to hold out my hand. When I did it, she placed three diamond rings in my hand, one of which was an engagement ring. At first I didn't know what I was looking at; but when I focused on the size of the rock in the engagement ring, I knew I'd seen it twice. Once at Tiffany's, and again when I was begging my man not to walk out my life. So I knew exactly who they belonged to I just wondered how they got em'.

"How the fuck did ya'll get these?!" I laughed observing them closely.

"Let's just say his pretty little girlfriend, ain't pretty no more," Mercedes said.

"Yeah.....a few days after that thing happened to Carissa, we blamed that bitch for it. We figured if Thick was in the picture, you wouldn't be all messed up and shit, and would be on your job. So we took our frustrations out on her. I think Dyson and them know we had somethin' to do with it, but we been denying it." Kenyetta laughed.

"So what ya'll robbed her or something?" I asked.

"Fuck no! What we look like robbing her ass? Her money

can't fuck wit ours! We sliced her fucking face up and took her rings as proof." Mercedes laughed.

"Is she alive?"

"Yep. But she paralyzed. And she will never look the same that's for sure," Kenyetta added.

"Damn ya'll some fuckin' pitbulls!"

We laughed.

Mercedes said, "But you ain't heard the worst part."

"I didn't?"

"Naw…The bitch lied about being pregnant. She probably ruined your relationship over telling Thick some bullshit and she wasn't even pregnant." Mercedes laughed.

That hurt. I was happy that my friends handled business for me, because I would've done it for them. But knowing that my world was ruined on the strength of a lie, tore me apart inside.

My curiosity was peaked. "How do you know she lied about being pregnant?"

"Well….when Thick asked the doctor if his baby was gonna be okay, he looked at him like he was fuckin' crazy. So he found out right then that, that bitch was a fuckin' liar!"

"So what he do?"

"Dropped a few G's for her hospital bill and left her ass stranded. He pissed 'bout that shit," Carissa added. "You know how bad he wants a kid."

"Yeah…that's why he loves L'il C so much!" Mercedes added.

I knew I shouldn't be, but I was happy that his world ended in a matter of seconds, like mine did. For some reason that news gave me the strength, I needed to resume my position in Emerald City. As far as I was concerned, he got exactly what he deserved.

"Well what's going on with Emerald City?" I asked.

They were real quiet before answering. I could tell by the looks in their eyes, that they needed me back just as much as I needed them.

"Shit ain't been the same. I had to kill Key because him and his brothers were gettin' ready to rape Carissa. If it hadn't been for Derrick coming back, I don't know what would've happened," Mercedes said.

"Derrick?" I asked, not believing my ears.

"Yes. Derrick. He really looked out girl," Mercedes said smiling a little more than she should have.

"Them niggas got us fucked up!" I said trying to wrap my mind around someone hurting one of my girls. "I'm just happy you're okay."

"Don't worry about it," Carissa said again. "I'm as tough as nails!"

"I know Lavelle flipped didn't he?" I questioned.

"Yeah...but I already handled it!" Mercedes told me proudly. "But they did air out everybody else in that mothafucka just for not stopping it."

"So you finally got a body on your gun?" I giggled. "Look at you, tryin' to be gangsta."

"Naw...I'm not gangsta, I'm cute! But I will fuck somebody up about my girls."

It was silent for a minute as I looked at all of them.

"Let's make a pact. That we'll always have each other's back from this moment forward." I put my hand in the middle and all of theirs covered mine.

"Nobody can break our bond!" Kenyetta said looking at all of us.

"Nobody!" Mercedes and Carissa added.

Our hands dropped after we fortified our friendship.

"Well...now that that's out the way. Let's get shit back in order. I'm back now!"

CHAPTER 19
WHAT'S UP
JANUARY, SATURDAY, 6:00 P.M.

THICK

Thick couldn't believe that Zakayla had lied to him about being pregnant.

He had plans to wife her and give her everything she wanted. He had already spent big money on the luxury apartment, the diamonds on her fingers, the clothes in her closet, and her truck. However, nothing proved his love more than dumping longtime girlfriend and business partner Yvette. But after finding out she was nothing but a liar, he felt the only thing he owed to her was paying her hospital bills.

He was on his way to check out the affairs at Emerald City, when he noticed Yvette outside running business. He smiled a little because he hadn't seen her in weeks. What caught him off guard was not how she was putting niggas in check, and handling business, but how good she looked. He could tell she'd lost a lot of weight and now she looked like she did when he first met her.

"I'm not tryin' to hear dat shit! Now you know your fuckin hours, and I expect you to be on your job!" Yvette yelled as she grabbed the hood of his coat.

"Yvette, I missed three days man. That was it!"

"I don't give a fuck. Since I been in charge of security, yo ass only been out of work one time. Now all of a sudden you need three days?! Don't fuck wit' me, Veil! Now get back to work." She was scolding one of Harold's soldiers.

He walked off and did as he was told. The soldiers realized that unlike the other women, Yvette wouldn't waste no time putting somebody in check or pulling the trigger. Her feistiness and the weight she lost began to turn Thick on.

He parked his truck in front of Unit C, and walked toward her. When Yvette saw Thick she started off in the other direction. She wasn't prepared to see him. Not yet. He quickly grabbed her hand before she was able to make it up the stairs. He knew if she made it inside her friends would be in her ear telling her to leave his sorry ass alone.

"Come here for a sec, Vette."

"I gotta go." She tried to pull away but his grip was tight.

"Where you goin?" he asked.

"Me and you ain't got nothin' to talk 'bout, Thick. It's over remember?"

"Look...I fucked up okay. I was wrong for even tryin' to play you. I let that bitch get in my head and I gotta live with the possibility of losing you. But I swear I'm ready to do right by you."

His words heavy in passion, caught her off guard and she so desperately wanted to believe him. But deep in her heart, she knew she couldn't.

"Thick why you doin' this to me? Please let me get on with my life." Tears ran down her face. "Do you know how hard it was for me to move on? Why can't you let me go?"

"Because I love you that's why. Come talk to me in my truck," he said trying to get her away from the watchful eyes of her friends.

"I can't Thick." She attempted to walk away again.

"Yvette please...just gimmie one minute." He begged

looking into her eyes.

It was the first time in a long time she heard the passion in his voice.

"Okay. Only for a minute," she conceded.

When she got in his truck, the familiar sight and smells snatched her back to a time when things were good with them. *Maybe we can work on it.* She thought. *Maybe he really does love me.*

When he came around to the driver's side of the car, he jumped in, closed the door, and pulled around the back of the building. The smell of the Touch cologne by Burberry he wore made her want to take him in her mouth. He let his five o'clock shadow come through, and shaped it up adding a distinguished look to a handsome thug. She couldn't help but stare at him, and admire how sexy he made a pair of jeans, Timbs, black shirt, and Coogi jacket look.

Before she could say anything, he reached in and kissed her. For a minute, she inhaled him then moved into his kisses. Her pussy began to throb as her heart was getting rid of what it had told her for the past few weeks. Here she was, smelling him, touching him and she didn't want it to end. Some kind of way, she managed to pull away from him, not wanting to give in too easy, not yet anyway.

"What's wrong baby?" he asked. "I said I was wrong for what I did to you. That bitch got in my head and fucked shit up. But I knew all along you were the woman for me. And I ain't neva lettin' that shit happen again. That's my word baby," he said touching her leg and sending chills through her.

"You hurt me, Thick. You hurt me bad. Do you know how it felt to see you walk arm and arm with another woman? You acted like you didn't even know me. Like I had done something to you. You couldn't even spend five minutes to tell me why it was over between us."

"I know. But you know how much I been wanting a baby. That bitch told me she was pregnant and I fell for it."

"Yeah but you cheated on me too! With all the shit that happened, you making me forget about that. You cheated on me, Thick. She shoulda never been able to pretend to be pregnant in the first fucking place!" Tears fell from her eyes.

"I know baby. That's why I'm glad ya'll fucked that bitch up, otherwise I'da married that scandalous hoe."

"Thick I didn't know nothing 'bout that," she said as she wiped the tears from her face. "Don't get me wrong, I'm glad she got what she deserved, but I didn't give the word on that shit either. I had made up my mind that you were gonna do what you wanted to do. And there was nothing I could do 'bout it."

She didn't want him thinking that she was so desperate to be with him, that she gave the order.

"Well whatever," he said. "I'm just glad it was done. But I do love you. Let's move on from this, and work on us baby." He gently grabbed her face and kissed her lips.

Yvette's heart started to beat rapidly. When Thick moved his body close to hers, and reached across her body to push her seat all the way back the anticipation of making love to him consumed her. She didn't think he deserved her body, but she couldn't resist him either. It was like he owned her, as if she still belonged to him. He unbuttoned her coat and gripped her breasts. She gave into his touches and confirmed her feelings by soft moans.

"I want to make love to you baby. I miss this pussy so much. Remember how we use to make love in my truck? Let's take things back to the way they use to be."

His words sent a wave of rage over her as she remembered him sleeping with Zakayla in his truck. Her hate took over when she thought about how she begged him not to leave, and he played her in front of all of her friends.

"You love me?" she asked as she breathed heavily into his kisses.

"Yes baby. I fuckin' love you girl," he said, his mouth covering hers and his dick reaching full thickness.

She moaned into his mouth. "Do you need me?"

"Yes baby I need you.....I need you."

She pulled away, startling him. "Well you should have thought about that before you walked out of my life. It's over. Go fuck that gimp in the hospital bed. I'm through wit' you!" She got out the car, slammed the truck door and ran toward the building.

After three unsuccessful attempts to get her to come back, Thick decided that he wasn't gonna be played. He noticed that in her rush to leave, she dropped her keys on his floorboards. He picked them up and devised a cold plan that would mean death, and ending his friend's relationships with their women.

Thick pulled up on an unsuspecting Critter in the alley behind Unit A. Even though it was dark, he'd knew the small framed Critter anywhere. As high as he'd gotten over the years he'd never lost his glasses and he always wore a dirty suit and dress coat like he was still working for the government. Thick could tell he was trying to cop some dope and the dealer he was talking to was giving him a hard time. *That nigga always want a freebie.* Thick thought. He knew his plan would work because Critter was fiening.

"Critter! Come here man," Thick yelled from his truck.

Critter moved as fast as he could to the truck, even though

121

the withdrawals were making things hard on his body.

Critter immediately started explaining. "Hey man. I ain't botherin' nobody, honest."

"Calm down nigga. I gotta job for you. You wanna make a couple of bucks?"

"Yeah. Sure man."

"Look…you gonna need some help. You got anybody that can help you bring some boxes down to my truck."

Critter looked around and saw Rod talking to another fiend in the yard. He flagged him down and they both stood at the passenger side of Thick's truck. Thick told them that he needed them to get his box from A55, which was one of the stash houses in Unit A. Thick gave them the Yvette's key and told them to get a box marked Thick's things. When they returned, he promised to give them dope and $50.00 a piece.

Critter and Rod eagerly accepted the keys and hurried up to Unit A to get the box. With their judgment clouded, and all they could think of was getting that dope and satisfying their high. When they got off the elevator, they ran down the hall toward A55. When they reached the door, Critter grabbed the key from his pocket and opened the door. Rod followed behind him and moved into the apartment.

The moment Kristina saw Critter and Rod coming through door she removed both of her guns from their holsters and unloaded multiple bullets in their body. Critter, although riddled with bullets, tried to crawl out of the apartment.

"Please…please don't kill me. Thick—"

Before he could get his sentence out, Kristina walked over top of him, and put two caps in his face.

When she was sure they were both dead, she picked up the keys off the floor, and noticed they were Yvette's.

Afterwards, she put in a call.

CHAPTER 20
WHAT'S UP
JANUARY, SUNDAY, 11:45 A.M.

CAMERON

"I'm tellin' you this is some bullshit. Yvette would have never given Critter her set of keys. She must've dropped them or somethin' baby."

"You think I don't know that?!" Cameron asked Mercedes in their bedroom.

"So what's gonna happen now?"

"We gonna have a meeting tonight. But you know shit is tight again since we got those extra bodies on us. That's over three bodies in three weeks. Five-O gonna be on our shit hard."

"I know. Damn!!"

"But don't worry 'bout nothin'." Cameron reached in and gave her a kiss. "As long as we have each otha, we straight."

"Is that right?" Mercedes smiled.

"That's right. Now you know I talked to my baby girl Chante right?"

"Naw. You didn't tell me." Mercedes said as she rubbed his shoulders. "Well what happened? Did you find out why her ass been cuttin' up in school?"

"Yep! She say we don't spend no time with her for one. And for two, she said her friends been clownin' her about

123

your moms fuckin' their grandpop's behind their grandma's back."

"You lyin! She said that?"

"I wish I was. So she felt she had to defend the family. So my l'il shawty was about to knife a muthafucka!"

"But the teacher baby?"

"She said that bitch ain't do nothin' to help when she told her they were teasin' her. So she flipped on her ass. I don't blame her either." Cameron laughed.

"It's this area baby. We got to get from around here," Mercedes said, looking at her engagement ring.

"We will." He kissed her ring. "Just as soon as we get married. But for now, we'll look into some private schools."

"Okay."

"And where's L'il C? He been out the house more than me lately."

"Out there on the yard with his friends. Leave him alone, he just tryin' to be like you." She smiled.

"I know right. My l'il nigga just like me." He stood up and put on his bulletproof vest. "Well let me see what's up with this meeting. I'll let you know the status the moment I hear something."

"I love you." She reached in for a kiss.

"I love you more." He grabbed one of her nipples and squeezed it. "I'm fuckin' them walls up when I get back tonight."

"Promises promises."

"And look. Tell Yvette everything will be okay and to keep her head up. We in this thing together."

"I will. But we all feelin' fucked up 'bout Critter. Kristina had to do what she had to do but he really looked out for us."

"I know baby." He hugged her. "But business is business and he ain't had no business bein' in our stash house either."

"You right."

"Well I'm on my way to this meeting. Keep my plate warm and my pussy tight," he said as he left out.

"What you sayin', Thick? Cuz what you tellin' me don't make no fuckin' sense man." Cameron yelled at the emergency meeting held at Thick's mother's place off of Minnesota Avenue in N.E.

"I'm sayin' that Yvette put our entire operation in jeopardy by wearin' her feelin's on her sleeve man. And if Kristina hadn't been on point, who knows how much money we woulda been into Dreyfus for," Thick said as he drank Absolute Pear on the rocks.

"I understand why you may be upset, but I'm in love with Carissa man. We been lookin' at new places to live and everything. Last week we put a deposit down on a new apartment out in Forestville Maryland. So what you tellin' me now don't even make no sense," Lavelle said.

"And when were you gonna tell us you were takin' one of the girls out of Emerald?" Thick asked.

"Soon," Lavelle said realizing his oversight.

"That's the kinda shit I'm talkin' about. This entire operation is fallin' the fuck apart!"

Thick was unsympathetic with his friends and their reasoning for not wanting to end their relationships. He felt what needed to be done, needed to be done even if he was the one that set Yvette up. For his own selfish reasons, he wanted them to end the relationships with their girlfriends, and pledge loyalty to Emerald City and Emerald City only. But what he hadn't expected was so much resistance, especially considering a few of them slept with other women on a regular basis the same way he did.

He hit his fist on the table and walked around it eyeing each of the members of the squad. "Listen....what would have happened if it had been somebody else runnin' up in the house?! Dreyfus woulda came in blazin just like he did on Tyland! And here ya'll are sittin' here cryin' over some bitches who'll probably leave ya'll asses in a couple of months anyway! Now if ya'll are loyal to anything, other that Emerald City, let me know. Cuz right now I'm confused. Maybe we'll have to revisit who'll be runnin' things in Emerald City."

"And what the fuck is that supposed to mean!" Dyson asked as he stood up.

"Just what the fuck I said!" Thick shot back. "Now I want to know right here and right fuckin' now, what the fuck do ya'll plan to do. Pledge loyalty to Emerald City by ending the relationships with the bitches that could ruin us and focus on business at hand?" He paused. "Or go on with what you doin' and risk somethin' worse happenin', the next time one of them gets mad."

The room fell silent.

Thick asked, "By a show of hands. Who's in and who's out? The time is now."

No one made a move until Dyson drank from his cup, wiped his hand on his jeans, looked at his brothers in blood, sweat and tears, and raised his hand.

"I pledge loyalty to ya'll," Dyson said.

Thick looked around the room, placed his gun on the table and said, "I'll lay down my life for every one of you muthafuckas!"

After that, Cameron and Lavelle both looked at one another searching for who would betray the woman they loved first. Because unlike the others, they intended to place the women in their lives on their arms. Lavelle quickly swallowed all of the drink in his glass and poured another glass. With as much hesitation and hurt as a man who didn't want to walk away from someone he loved could muster, he reluctantly raised his hand.

"I pledge loyalty to my brothers too. Don't let me down."

Cameron was fucked up when Lavelle folded because he realized he was the only other person outside of himself, who loved his woman. But Cameron also knew the day would one day come, where he too would have to choose. But he never knew it would happen so soon. So without wasting any more time, he made his decision.

"I pledge Honor, Loyalty, Obedience and Silence to the Emerald City Squad, always."

For the next hour, they devised a plan that would keep the women in office permanently, and dissolve their relationships completely over the next six months. They figured if they'd gotten use to working for them as opposed to being in a relationship nothing like what happened to Yvette would happen again. They were convinced by what Thick was telling them, that they could convince the women that a strictly business relationship was best for everyone.

Thick didn't share with him his own selfish motives for wanting them to end their relationships. All he ever wanted was control, and control over everything. He wanted control over Yvette, and when he couldn't get it, he ran to Zakayla. He wanted control over Zakayla, but when he felt she betrayed him, he left her stranded and tried to run back to Yvette. But when Yvette saw right through him, he plotted against her.

But Thick's evil plot started long ago when he wanted control over Emerald City so he placed the order to have Dex and his wife Stacia killed.

At this point, all he wanted to do was run Emerald City and reap its benefits.

No matter who he had to hurt in the process.

CHAPTER 21
STILL TRUE
FEBRUARY, SATURDAY, 9:15 A.M.

DOCTANIAN

Doctanian was inside his girlfriend's wet pussy.

He was trying desperately not to reach an orgasm so quickly, but ever since she became pregnant, the walls of her pussy became tighter and hotter. Prior to now, he always thought it was just a rumor that pregnant pussy felt so good.

He was stroking Jordan's pussy repeatedly when he felt his self sliding into a euphoric orgasm.

He let out a moan. "I'm cummin' baby."

"Cum on daddy. Cum inside this wet pussy." She urged. "I want to feel you inside me."

Without saying another word, Doctanian let himself go, as he oozed all of his cum inside of her heated pussy. When he pulled out, Jordan lifted her body and placed his warm dick inside her mouth.

"Ummmmm. I love to taste you after you've been inside of me."

It was this type of thing that made him obsess over Jordan. While she had him still inside of her mouth, sucking him as if she was licking a piece of candy, her cell phone rang like it had several times earlier in the day. He started to ignore it but on instinct, he reached on the nightstand to give it to her to prevent Jordan from straining her pregnant body to grab it herself. She jumped up, and snatched it out of his hand.

"I got it!" she said as she ran to the bathroom and closed the door behind her.

"Okay. If it's one of your little friends, tell 'em thanks for fuckin' shit up!" He laughed, as he lay on the bed naked and satisfied.

He was in love with her in every sense of the word. Now after five months of her being pregnant, he was preparing to propose to her and move her out of Emerald City before the baby was born.

Doctanian jumped up and knocked on the door after realizing Jordan was still on the phone twenty minutes later. He wasn't trying to be jealous, but he thought lately her behavior was sort of weird. When she came out, he asked her was everything okay. She brushed him off and said it was a friend who had something going on with her family. After taking one look at her beautiful naked body, and the belly that was carrying his baby, he melted instantly.

"I'm sorry Shawty. Let me get out here and make some cash so I can get you out this hood."

"No problem daddy," Jordan said as she kissed him sucking gently on this bottom lip. "I got a little treat for you when you come back over."

Doctanian got dressed and left Jordan's apartment in Emerald City, which she shared with her mother who was also his customer.

Doctanian wasn't sure at first, but after awhile he was positive he saw L'il C serving somebody. This bothered him because although he put in work for his father, he always

131

hoped L'il C would stand clear of the game. When the customer left, Doctanian hurried over to him before he got a chance to serve anybody else.

"Ay man! What you doin' out here!"

"Same thing you doin'!" L'il C said as he pulled down his cap and added his money in his pile.

"But why you doin' it? Your family already paid."

"Cuz I want my own dough! You live off your folks?"

"Naw! But if they were livin' it up like yours and I was still a youngin' I damn sure would be."

"Well everything ain't what it look like," L'il C said in a low voice. "My folks ain't together no more. They don't think I know but I do. Anyway.......I'm old enough to make my own way now."

Doctanian didn't like hearing L'il C talking like he was but figured it would happen sooner or later if his parents didn't get a better grip on him.

"Listen L'il nigga, whatever happened to you bein' that video director we talked 'bout?" Doctanian asked.

"Naw. I changed my mind. My friends think that's whack."

"That's cuz they some pussies. Only pussies would think being a video director is whack. Do you realize how many women you'd be around any given day?" Doctanian asked as he play punched him in the face. "This life ain't for you man."

"Why not? You do it," L'il C asked.

Doctanian didn't know what to say because at that point in his life, he was living fucked up. He hated serving dope and seeing the effects everyday it took on customer's bodies. His mother's words haunted him every day when she said what he was doing was wrong. And although she didn't think he was listening, he was. But he was saving his money to eventually move his girlfriend, baby and mother out of the hood. To him it was just a matter of time.

"You right. I ain't neva lied to you and I ain't gonna start now. So let's do this. You become a big time video director and I'll produce you. We'll be like them punk ass niggas Jay Z and Dame Dash was."

L'il C looked up in the air as if he was seriously thinking about his offer. And then the same smile came across his face that Doctanian had seen before when he was sure he'd won him over. And in a way, he wished it was easy for him to believe in dreams just as easy as it was for L'il C too. No matter what, he made up his mind to keep any promise to him he made, just as long as he took the offer, and stayed out the game.

"Okay! We gotta a deal!" L'il C said as he gave him five.

"Alright! But I don't wanna see you out here no more unless you comin' to see me."

"I know man! Stop sweatin' me."

"Ahn Ahn man. Before you go I want to know somethin'."

"What man?!" L'il C asked.

"Who put you on anyway?"

L'il C turn around and said, "Uncle Thick."

Doctanian couldn't believe his ears.

CHAPTER 22

THE MEETING
JANUARY, SATURDAY, 6:00 P.M.

YVETTE

After three weeks, I was finally able to convince my girls to go out with me on a night on the town.

After they said no to dancing, we settled for drinks instead. And when we stepped out, we looked like we were getting ready to shoot a music video. We were dressed in Fatigues, and different color wife beaters and we all were wearing make-up. Every dude in there was trying to holla the moment we walked through the bar.

"So what's this 'bout, Yvette?" Mercedes asked. "You been askin' us out for a while now and now we're here and you ain't sayin' nothin'."

"I'm just happy to see ya'll that's all. Plus I wanted you to get some liquor up in you before I get down to business."

"Well if you don't mind, I'd like to get down to business now," Carissa said.

"Me too," Mercedes added.

"May I take your orders now? Or would you like refills on your drinks?" the waitress asked.

We were posted up at the Dave & Buster's in White Flint. I was able to reserve the private room for us at the last minute, because I felt for what needed to be said, needed to be done in private.

"Yes please. Bring everybody a double of everything. And come back for our orders later."

"No problem," she said as she walked off, eyeing the five crisp $100 dollar bills already lying on the table.

"So what's up girl?" Mercedes asked.

"Okay. Has anybody noticed a difference in the guys?" I asked in a low voice, as I sipped on my Vodka martini.

They looked around at one another, and then back at me. Carissa decided to speak first.

"Have we noticed a change in the guys? Is that some kind of fuckin' trick question or somethin'?"

"No it's not, Rissa. I'm very serious."

"If you consider Lavelle not coming home, and tellin' me he don't know about the relationship anymore after he's all I known different, hell yes! Or if you call him comin' by checkin' on me like he's my fuckin' manager instead of my boyfriend, then yes! I consider that different too. Or if you call bein' different, him comin' by kissin' the girls and ignorin' the hell out of me, then I guess we got somethin' too! So you tell me, Yvette, what do you fuckin' think?!" she screamed as Kenyetta rubbed her gently on the back trying to hold back her own tears.

"Yvette, you're our girl and we love you. But we have business to run at Emerald City, so we need to know what's up. Askin' stuff like this is only makin' matters worse. If you got somethin' to say just say it. Be real with us. Whatever it is, we can handle it." Kenyetta said as she handed Carissa a napkin for her tears.

"I think they planned this," I finally said, looking at all of them. I wanted to see if they felt anything remotely similar to what I felt.

Mercedes asked, "Planned what?"

"I think they planned to dump us. Now I don't know 'bout Thick. I believe in my heart that nigga was doin' what the fuck he was doin' anyway. But you not goin' to tell me that Lavelle is gonna up and leave you Carissa and that all of a sudden, Cameron, who loves your dirty draws girl, will all of a sudden leave you too, at the same time!"

"But what sense does that make?" Mercedes insisted.

"Exactly. It makes no fuckin' sense! All of this is some bullshit! We laid our lives on the line. No, scratch that! We LAY our lives on the line EVERY FUCKIN' DAY FOR THEM NIGGAS! And them muthafuckas swore, that this shit would never be permanent, and that they'd come back for us when it was all said and done. And what did they do? Dump us at the first sign of trouble."

When I looked around at my sister's faces, I could tell I was getting to them, and I decided to hit the hammer on the nail.

"I believe what happened between me and Thick triggered everythin'. I believe by me abandoning, Emerald City, that gave them the impression, that we couldn't handle a relationship and business at the same time."

"This ain't your fault girl," Kenyetta said.

"I didn't say that," I said. "I don't believe this is any of our faults. I believe we're victims of our love to niggas who didn't deserve it. And I believe we played the fool for men who promised to protect us and didn't."

When the waitress returned with our drinks, I advised her that she was very helpful, but unless we called her back, we wouldn't be needing her anymore for the rest of the night. I didn't want any other witnesses around for what was about to be said.

"So what's up girl? We've been knowin' you far too long. Somethin's gotta be up. What's your plan?" Kenyetta asked.

"I say we overthrow them and take over Emerald City."

It was so silent now the only sound that could be heard was the crowd in the game room. I was surprised because although I would've never thought about betraying my man, in my mind I still knew we could run Emerald City alone if we needed to. We were doing it anyway. But their silence only proved to me that they didn't feel the same.

"Do you know what you're sayin'?" Carissa asked.

"You damn right I do!"

"We can't do that?" Carissa laughed as she threw back both of her drinks. "Can we?"

"Why not?" Mercedes asked, looking around the table. "Why can't we?"

That's what I'm talkin' about! My girl's are finally waking up! I thought to myself.

"I was thinkin' the same thing," Kenyetta added. "We've been runnin' Emerald City all along anyway. And since them muthafuckas want to carry it like that, let 'em get carried!"

"There go my muthafuckin' girls!" I smiled.

"What 'bout Dreyfus? He got a relationship wit' them?" Carissa asked.

"Dreyfus has a relationship wit' his money. The only thing he worried 'bout is getting' paid. He don't care 'bout nothin' else. Anyway you think he don't know we're the gatekeepers? You think if somethin' happened to Emerald City's stash, he wouldn't come to us first?" I asked.

"She right 'bout that shit! He'd walk over our bodies to get to theirs." Mercedes laughed.

"But he's the connect. How can we use the connect—"

I cut Carissa off and answered all her questions at once. I had already quarterbacked the entire thing before I even came to them. There's one thing I didn't like to do and that was come to a meeting with a bunch of bullshit. I always came prepared and with a plan in mind. Thick taught me that.

"This is how it's goin' down," I said as they all moved in to listen. "The first thing we do is move out of Emerald City."

"But they'll know somethin's up," Carissa said.

"No they won't. Just like Yvette moved all her shit without movin' shit out the building, that's the same way we can move," Kenyetta said. "I don't need shit in that apartment."

"Speak for yourself bitch." Mercedes laughed. "I need my fur coats."

I told them. "Well this is what we do. We take as much stuff by hands as we can. No boxes and no trash bags. Then we keep the apartments. They'll come in handy later. Trust me. We change the locks too because them niggas got keys, we want them cut the fuck off."

"I'm likin' this shit more and more already," Kenyetta said in a devious tone.

"Once we're moved out, we give away testers for the entire week the guys go away to Vegas. This will force us to have to contact Dreyfus to get more supply. At this point Mercedes and I will meet with Dreyfus and build a rapport. It'll be us because Mercedes is familiar with the weight since she collects the money from the lieutenants, and I'm in charge of security.

"Once we make him comfortable, we'll get in good with the lieutenants and the soldiers. We'll feel out who's who. Now I already predict they'll be a problem with two of the lieu's and their soldiers. They're too loyal to the niggas. If we have to, we'll kill 'em. Does anybody got a problem with that?"

"Wit' what?" Carissa asked.

"Murder."

"I'll die for ya'll," Carissa said.

"I'll die for ya'll too," Kenyetta said.

"I already killed a muthafucka so it ain't nothin' but a thang." Mercedes bragged.

Everyone laughed.

"I ain't gotta say shit because ya'll know I'll lay a muthafucka on their backs twice quick for my girls. So if we ain't got no problem with that, it's all good. When the niggas come back from Vegas, there will be some drama, believe that. But they got other shops, so if they're smart they can gracefully bow down. Plus we'll have our soldiers already rearranged and ready for war."

"This wild ass shit just might work!" Carissa said smiling.

"This wild ass shit *will* work," I said. "Cuz they broke their promise and did us grimy and pay back is a bitch."

"You know we gonna have to kill Thick right?" Mercedes asked seriously. "He ain't gonna just roll over and give up EC."

"No....I'm gonna have to kill Thick. And I'm just the bitch to do it."

CHAPTER 23
GREED
FEBRUARY, FRIDAY, 7:34 P.M.

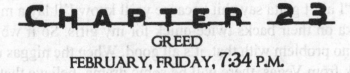

"Come on, Jordan! What the fuck you waitin' on?" Erick yelled.

"I ain't neva done nothin' like this before, Erick. You gotta give me some more time." She cried on the cell phone in her room, hoping no one could hear the dirt she was planning against the one man who loved her more than himself.

"You ain't gotta do nothin' but have his ass come to your house. Me and my boys doin' the rest. If anythin' you lookin' out for your man, so we won't put this lead in 'em'!"

"My boy and your lieutenant." She reminded him while sitting on her bed.

"Fuck that shit! Ain't nobody bossin' me around. Shit gonna start changin' for real. I just need you to do what we agreed on."

"But....but then he'll lose his position as lieutenant. They'll know he let somebody get into the building and that he wasn't on watch." Jordan sniffed as she began to gather the covers in a bunch between her legs wiping her tears with them.

"Listen, Jordan...Emerald City is gettin' ready to fold anyway. You ain't notice Thick and 'em, ain't been around here lately?"

"Yeah but—"

"But what?!" He shot back getting upset that she was wasting too much time. "I got connects set up at Tyland Towers where if this goes through, I'm gonna be lieutenant and maybe even captain. And if you do this, you'll be securing Doc's future so he won't have to mop no floors at Wal-Mart. Think about your baby!"

"I am!" she yelled. "That's why I'm scared!"

Erick was in Jordan's ear hard. He had been trying to convince her for over two weeks, to help him get Doctanian to leave his shift early, which was something he never did. Erick knew that it was just a matter of time before the stash houses changed again, and because he didn't have his connect who told him where the new houses moved, once this one changed again, he wouldn't know about anymore. And if that happened, he couldn't plot to rob another house.

He needed Jordan's help in the worse way if this was gonna to work right. Erick knew that the lieutenants operated the front of the Units with the soldiers; therefore, only one soldier manned a stash house inside the building during shop hours. This was because extra security was already outside the building and was deemed unnecessary. So his plan was to send to unsuspecting dummies ahead of him first to break inside the stash house.

Whoever was on guard would eradicate them immediately, but wouldn't see Erick coming or the bullet he'd placed in their head. In order for his plan to work, it had to be done before shop hours ended, because they increased security afterwards with three or four soldiers guarding at a time.

"Okay." Jordan sniffled. "How much you given me again?" she asked. She was hurt, but not enough *not* to claim the money he said he'd give her.

"You funny. I'm gonna give you four G's. Like I said." He laughed feeling comfortable that she was going to help him again.

"Okay….but don't hurt my baby's father. If you don't see him walkin' toward my buildin', call this shit off!" Jordan demanded.

"Your baby daddy huh? Now that's funny. How you know you ain't carryin' my kid around in there?"

His words caused Jordan to press the end button on her cell phone, and throw it across her room against her bedroom door. She always thought he could possibly be the father, but the thought alone was as disgusting as Doctanian not being the father. She only slept with Erick because he was aggressive and cocky and at times that turned her on. But when the sex was over, she always wished she hadn't shared her body with him because he was always so rude and disrespectful to her. With Doc she had a future, with Erick she knew she'd have nothing.

Having heard the thump against her daughter's bedroom door, Jordan's mother Da'vanta walked into the room without knocking, something Jordan hated and asked her what was wrong.

"Ma get outta of here!" Jordan yelled trying to prevent her from seeing her red face, which just moments before, was crying.

"You okay baby?" she asked trying to soften her up, so she could hopefully cop some dope from Doctanian later if he was coming over. Doctanian fed her needs sometimes, but he started to hate it considering she was his girlfriend's mother.

"Yeah, Ma! Please leave! I want to be alone."

"You sure baby? Want me to make you some tea or somethin'?" she asked, rubbing her arms.

"No, get outta of here!"

Da'vanta was on her way out the door when she bent her frail body down to pick up her daughter's ringing cell phone. She became instantly upset when she noticed it was Erick's name across the display. She handed it to her daughter, who snatched it out of her hands instantly and demanded that she leave her room.

"Ma get out!"

"I'm still your mother!" she said as she slammed the door and walked to her dark dim living room, wondering when her next fix would come.

Da'vanta hated Erick because she felt he had something to do with the only man she ever loved being killed. But the love of her life was also responsible for getting her hooked on dope.

She couldn't help but cry as she thought about Critter.

CHAPTER 24

LOYALTY

FEBRUARY, SATURDAY, 9:18 P.M.

In the past Doctanian had been kidnapped and held at gunpoint and yet he never felt fear any fear like the fear he felt right now.

Upon receiving the news that his girlfriend Jordan might be having a miscarriage, he ran to his most trusted soldier Erick, and asked him to hold down the fort, while he saw about the love of his life.

"Look man! I need you to look afta' things real quick!" Doctanian said as he tried to prevent himself from breaking down. "I gotta go handle somethin' now!"

"No problem man. Everything cool?" Erick asked, curious as to see what lie Jordan told him, that had him so shook.

"Naw man. Between me and you, my girl may be havin' a miscarriage. I don't know what I'ma do if she loses the baby. I love them more than I love myself! That's my word!" Doc said, trying to hold back how he felt, although it showed through stronger than any words he could say.

Miscarriage? Erick thought. *Damn that bitch is good!*

"I got you man," he said while placing in his hand on Doc's back. "I got these niggas out here. Go and take care of you and yours. Shit is all good out here! I got these niggas on lock. Trust!" Erick said as he convinced Doc to abandon his post.

With that, Doctanian ran toward his girlfriend's building. *Sucker for love ass nigga!* Erick thought as he gave the word to the others that the plan was being carried out.

Out of breath and worried, Doc banged on Jordan's door. When her mother answered, he was angry when she didn't appear as worried as a mother whose daughter was having a miscarriage should be.

"What's wrong Doc?!" Da'vanta asked sensing his eagerness to get in.

"Where's Jordan?!" he asked as he pushed his way through the door, and into Jordan's room.

"She ain't here," Da'vanta said. "I woke up and she was gone."

"She didn't tell you she was having a miscarriage?" he asked as he walked back into the living room with her. "She didn't say anything to you?"

"A *miscarriage*? No. She didn't say anything to me about havin' no miscarriage."

His mind was on overload as he assumed the ambulance had come in and rushed his girlfriend out of the house. While she was talking, he looked around for signs of disruption. He decided to calm down and question Da'vanta thoroughly. Maybe she'd seen more than she realized, but due to smoking dope she needed a jolt to make her remember.

"Ms. Porter, I'm worried 'bout Jordan. I need you to tell me everything that happened when she was here. Don't leave out nothin' because this is very important."

Ms. Porter realized that unlike any other boy her daughter dated, Doc genuinely cared about Jordan.

"Okay…well…" she said as she sat on the sofa. "Earlier she was in her room upset. I came in and saw her cell phone on the floor."

Doc's heart raced as he imagined her in pain and him not being there for her.

"So I came in and asked her what was wrong and if I could do anything for her." She rubbed her temples and then the sides of her arms.

"And what else, Ms. Porter?" He demanded attempting to jolt her as she nodded off. "Ms. Porter, what else?!"

"Oh….I'm sorry. And Erick," she said coming out of a dope induce nod. "Erick called and she took the call."

Doctanian backed up against the 32-inch TV on the stand knocking it over. The most treacherous thought imaginable ran through his mind. It sounded like his girlfriend and his child's mother was possibly setting him up.

He tried to run to the door but was slowed by the pain in his heart and the knots in his stomach. Feeling loyalty to Emerald City and being a true lieutenant, he decided to face his mistake head on; even if it meant losing his position or even his life.

He pulled out his cell phone and contacted the person he knew could hustle up the manpower needed to prevent whatever was getting ready to happen, and that was Yvette.

CHAPTER 25

CAN'T PLEASE EVERYBODY
JANUARY, SATURDAY, 6:00 P.M.

THICK

Vegas' night sky was a brilliant mixture of oranges and reds preparing for the sunset.

People were just waking up from their naps eager to stay up until the sun started all over again. No matter how much glitz and glamour was surrounding the Emerald City squad, there was still obvious tension in the air, causing the atmosphere to be tense.

"I don't understand why you would invite that bum bitch!" Lavelle yelled at Thick in the hallway of his suite at the Bellagio. "I don't fuck wit' that girl all like that."

The squad had reserved four rooms, with an extra room for the girls Thick decided to bring with them from the city. He called himself helping his friends get over Mercedes and Carissa, but Lavelle was growing irritated. Sharonda was in her room while Shannon stayed up under them in the hopes of catching any stray bills falling to the floor.

The squad was there mainly for business, because Thick had convinced them that it wasn't cool to live under the fear Dreyfus any longer, since several attempts to take down their stash houses in the past, would cause them more problems than it was worth. He was also tired of dealing with him on consignment for the weight he needed to keep the city moving. Although Dreyfus had made it clear that he'd be willing to accept his money up front, they had gotten use to the modest time frame he allowed to pay his money back, even though it came with jump in the price.

Thick was given a name of a Cuban connect who agreed to meet with the squad after hearing how easy they move weight in Emerald City. The connect offered to supply the weight at an affordable rate up front, and transport it safely to the city. After hearing this news, the fellas agreed that as long as they would be able to pay Dreyfus off, and sever the relationship on good terms, they'd be willing to meet Thick's connect.

"I thought you were feelin' her yo! I was tryin' to cheer your punk ass up because I'm tired of slippin' on your slob. You niggas been cryin' for three weeks and you startin' to bring me down!" he said as he walked into the living room where Cameron was receiving a shoulder massage by Shannon, Derrick's jump off.

"Man I'm not tryin' to be stuck in Vegas with Sharonda's ass all week. I fuck wit' her when I get ready to and leave it at that. Anyway, I thought the main purpose of this trip was business. They shouldn't even be here," Lavelle said, placing his nickel-plated .45 on the table.

"Look…..we can leave them bitches down here for all I give a fuck. It don't make me know neva mind," he said as he shrugged his shoulders and lit the blunt, acting like her friend Shannon wasn't even in the room. "I was just lookin' out for ya'll cryin' ass niggas."

"Man ain't nobody tryin' to leave them hoes down here," Lavelle said as he brushed what he considered to be a dumb ass comment off.

He didn't want to be bothered, but he wasn't trying to

carry no females like that, especially considering he had daughters and wouldn't want anybody treating them badly. He just didn't want his entire week ruined in Vegas.

"All I'm sayin is bringin' them females down here ain't gonna make me move or work no quicker," Lavelle said as he pulled on the blunt Thick handed him. "All she gonna do is make me mad."

Cameron wasn't saying much. He didn't understand why Thick invited the girls either. But after being up under a woman who took care of her body, and was as soft as Shannon, he was good for now. Still nobody could get his mind off Mercedes, he didn't care how good the pussy was.

"Yeah but maybe it'll help you get over that bitch!" Thick laughed as Cameron took time from his shoulder massage, to see what Lavelle's response would be.

"Be careful nigga that *bitch* you talkin' 'bout is still my daughter's mother. And if you call her out her name again, my loyalty to Emerald City ends here," he said as he put his finger on the table, which was close to his gun.

"You's a funny nigga." Thick laughed as he walked toward the door connecting the rooms and popped his collar. "Ya'll niggas so in love ya'll green. As long as it don't fuck wit' my business, it's all good."

He walked into his room and stuck his head back out the door. "Shannon," he barked.

"Yes," she answered, looking up from Cameron's neck to see what he needed.

"Come here."

Without saying another word, she disappeared into the room with him and closed the door behind her.

Leaving Cameron alone.

149

CHAPTER 26
STRAPPED
JANUARY, SATURDAY, 9:35 P.M.

"We got the back secure. I'm turning off this phone so it won't go off when we rush they asses in the hallway. Ya'll ready?" Derrick asked Yvette on the CB radio they used for emergency purposes only.

"Born ready nigga!"

Strapped with Glocks, Oozies and TEC-9's Derrick grabbed four of his *best* soldiers to secure the back of Until B, which was the building Doctanian manned. Doctanian had sent them to make sure everything was okay, after speaking to Jordan's mother. Something didn't sit with him right, and he wanted them to make sure.

Creeping up the steps quickly, but quietly, they had their guns in full view and ready to unload. An old lady trying to meet her friends on the 3rd floor for a game of Bingo, was entering from the fourth floor. She almost passed out when she saw them creeping up the stairs dressed in all black. There was no need to tell her not to say anything about what she'd seen, because they'd all ready seen her face. Running back from where she came, she gave her apologies for disturbing them, and disappeared.

The stash house was in Unit B, on the eighth floor. Any

other time walking up the steps would have taken an immediate toll on Derrick's crew, considering they weren't aerobic cats. But tonight they didn't need to be fit, to do what needed to be done. They were running strictly off adrenaline.

As they approached the eighth floor, their hearts were pounding with the anticipation of what was in store. Far from punks, his soldiers were ready to unleash on his command, and only his command. When Derrick heard footsteps, he placed his finger over his mouth quieting them.

When they stopped moving, they realized that in the stairwell above them were two sets of footsteps that sounded as if they were moving in their direction. Suddenly they stopped, when a door opened, and a third set of steps became present.

Some one spoke. "What the fuck ya'll doin' man?!"

Derrick believed it was Doctanian's right hand man Erick. "What you talkin' 'bout we—"

Erick cut them off. "I don't' want to hear that shit! Ya'll some thievin' ass niggas! And I can't stand thievin' ass niggas."

"What the…I'm confused as shit man. You need to tell me what the fuck is goin' on." The other voice echoed in the hallway. "We did everything—"

Before he could complete his statement, Derrick heard a bullet swirl from the barrel of what sounded like a .45 automatic weapon.

An anxious voice yelled out. "What the fuck you doin' man! Why you kill him like that?"

To see what was going on, Derrick instructed his troops to run full speed up the steps ready to lay down everybody if need be. When they reached the area where the voices were, they saw Ice, one of Doctanian's soldiers pointing a gun at the back of Erick's head. The noise from them running up the stairs, gave Ice the distraction he needed to catch Erick off guard and take his weapon.

Erick knew they were coming when he walked to Unit C and saw Derrick's boys manning the station instead of the girls. They hardly ever left their post. Immediately, he went to plan B to protect his name. The only reason he went over to Unit C in the first place was to be seen before he robbed the stash house. But he was glad he did. He figured if something went down, the girls could vouch that he wasn't involved. But when he didn't see them manning the post, he knew word had gotten out that somebody was trying to infiltrate. So he hustled over to the building not wanting his co-conspirators to be caught alive.

"Put your fuckin' gun down slim!" Ice yelled at Erick.

Erick complied and put his hands up in the air.

"Them to. Tell them to put their fuckin' guns down," Ice yelled.

"We ain't puttin' shit down so you can get that out your fuckin' head," Derrick said as he gave the signal to buck that nigga when he gave the okay. "Now I want to know what the fuck is goin' on!" Derrick asked eyeing Tonio's dead body.

"He a thief!" Erick interjected. He didn't care if he shot him or not, he still didn't want anybody knowing the part he took in everything.

"If I'm a thief, yo ass is a thief too nigga......believe that! You tryin' to set me up or somethin' Erick? Yeah. That's what you do," Ice said as he began to talk like a maniac. "This nigga's tryin to set me up."

"You talkin' shit nigga!" Erick screamed, realizing that his chances were better with calling him a liar and living than to take the beef that he was trying to rob the stash house too. Because either way, if they found out he was in on it, he was still going to die.

"I'm talkin' shit? I'm talkin' shit nigga?" Ice yelled as he pushed the barrel of the gun toward his head, forcing him against the wall. His back facing the closed door behind him.

"I don't know 'bout him talkin' shit, but you definitely are!" Yvette said as she busted through the sixth floor door and unleashed a .45 bullet inside Ice's skull. "I'm tired of these niggas fuckin' wit' my money," she said as she wiped the blood off her mouth with the back of her hand and looked at Derrick.

She saw everything from the small glass window in the door and waited patiently for the moment to pull the trigger.

"That was some sexy ass shit Shawty!" Derrick said as he put down his weapon, while instructing his soldiers to stay on guard.

"Thanks baby. I'm glad you liked it." She winked tucking her weapon in the back of her pants.

Suddenly Derrick smiled when he saw gun barrels sticking out as if Charlie's Angel's were coming through the doorway. His heart dropped when he saw Mercedes in a ski mask move into the hallway with Carissa and Kenyetta following. Only putting their weapons down, when they saw Derrick's boy was still pointing at Erick. He knew it was Mercedes because although she had the ski mask on, her ponytail peaked through with the streaked golden blonde hair that he liked.

"So it was true huh?!" Mercedes asked, removing her ski mask revealing her beautiful face. "Some niggas were tryin' to get us again?"

"Hold fast," Yvette said. "We ain't out the woods yet. What's the deal with this nigga?" Yvette asked Derrick, while looking at Erick.

"I don't know yet. Let's ask him," he said turning his attention to him. "What's your story? What you doin' here man?"

"I got word that somebody was tryin' to steal from the

house," he said huffing and puffing pretending he was out of breath. "So I came to see 'bout it."

"Is that right?" Yvette asked doubting every word he said. "And how the fuck you know where the house was at?"

Erick was so shook that he didn't stop to think about that before he ran off his mouth. He thought quick as Derrick's soldiers were ready to give the orders to end his life. "I came lookin' for Doc. His girl hit me up sayin' he wasn't there yet. When I did, I saw Derrick's soldiers at Unit C, and they told me ya'll went to see 'bout something over here."

"Which nigga was that?" Derrick asked, making mental notes to check whoever it was later.

"I can't remember man. It all happened so fast. You can ask 'em though."

"Oh we will." Derrick promised.

"Well I'm hearing' different stories," Yvette added. "I'm hearin' you fuckin' wit' Doctanian's bitch and ya'll tried to set us up."

Figuring that word must've gotten out that he talked to Jordan, he concocted another lie. He wasn't worried about Jordan vouching for his story, he had already pumped led in her body, and stuffed her in the dumpster around back. He made a promise the night CJ and Charles were killed, never to have witnesses, and he wanted to keep it that way.

"Like I said....Jordan called me tryin' to contact Doc because he wouldn't answer his phone. Ya'll know we use to kick it way back when and she still had my number. Ain't nothin' else to it, I swear!"

When it was obvious they didn't believe him, he went a bit further. "Ya'll can ask her right now." He continued, throwing up his hands for added effect.

Since the call placed to Yvette from Doctanian indicated something was not right, they decided to let him go. But

Derrick promised to finish him later if he found out anything different, and Erick had a feeling he had every intention to keep his promise.

Once again, Erick got away.

CHAPTER 27
CLOSING THE DEAL
FEBRUARY, WEDNESDAY, 3:45 P.M.

MERCEDES

Driving three hours to Dreyfus's compound in Virginia gave me some extra time to clear my mind and prepare for what needed to be done.

My goal was to convince the biggest dealer in D.C. that he should stop doing business the way he had been, and start doing things differently.

Yvette was able to get the number of the connect from the new Chief of Tyland Towers. She told him we were runnin' shit for the Emerald City squad, which was common knowledge to most people anyway. Stoney, the chief, ain't see nothing weird about givin' us the info when we told him we were running low and them niggas were in Vegas. The truth was we gave away testers and put our own money together before we even approached him.

I was amazed at how cool, calm and collected Yvette was about the whole matter. My girl was made for this life! Me? Well, I loved the glamour of it all but I could've done without the violence. But Yvette, she proved over and over that she was *more* than willing to do whatever needed to be done to takeover. I guess that's why I couldn't handle seeing her the way she was when Thick left her. It was like she was going through withdrawals. I couldn't help but wonder what was going on in her head now. Even though she seemed to be doing the best out of all of us.

Carissa cried every time somebody in the hood asked her about Lavelle. She would break down the minute his name was called. And Kenyetta had been acting as if she didn't have time for us outside of handling business. But it was cool though. We all had to deal with shit the best way we can.

As for me, Cameron was my life so I take my emotions out when I'm at home alone. Ain't no since in me adding to the burdens. I'm tryin' to be strong for Yvette, because sometimes I feel like she's holdin' shit down by herself.

"Shit girl!! This nigga Dreyfus is paid for real!" Yvette said as she looked out of the window and onto the four lush acres of land his property sat on.

In the middle of his circular driveway was a huge waterfall. His place was laid. The huge yard was flanked by streams and bordered by a lush green forest. This was definitely different from what we're use to seeing considering the only birds in the hood were pigeons

"I guess he would be livin' the life. Emerald City keeps his ass cozy with the price he charges on the weight."

"I know, I know. But that's why we need to stick to the plan," Yvette said as the butler immediately came to the car to greet us. "We're here for one purpose and one purpose only, to convince him that business will be *better* with us then it was with them."

"How 'bout I just let you do the talkin' since you're more talented in the oral department than I am." I laughed.

"You heard that rumor too?" Yvette laughed while walking up his huge steps leading to his double doors. "Yeah.....it's true. I do have skills. So let me handle this little girl. You just watch my flow and take notes." She continued as she patted me on my back holding the steel briefcase tightly in her hand.

Once inside we were awestruck at the limestone floors, oak paneling, vaulted ceilings and oversized fireplace. As with most drug kingpins, there were several beautiful women walking around wearing tiny miniskirts. Some were carrying trays that held drinks and nose candy. The butler took us to the rotunda where Dreyfus was drinking a glass of red wine. He looked much older and reserved than I envisioned him. If I saw him walking down the street, I would have pegged him for a senator instead of a king pin. Looking up over the glasses resting on his nose, he stood up, shook our hands and offered us a seat.

The room had a fireplace tucked away in the corner. The crackling from the fire filled the air considering he had yet to speak. His quiet nature put me on edge and I wanted to grab Yvette's hand and run out the door. We had a nerve thinkin' we could handle business on this level. The only thing that prevented me from running was the pencil skirt suit I was wearing. It was so tight I probably would've busted my ass tryin' to get out of there.

Yvette said we should rock the professional look so we both had to run out and buy dress suits, we had a few fly ass dresses in our closet, but nothing professional. I chose a white pencil skirt suit with the jacket buttoned all the way up no bra. My white pumps with the steel heel made the outfit classy but nasty. I turned shit out with my platinum necklace with the diamond drops.

Yvette was wearing a black form-fitting suit with a lace chemise under it. She looked vicious showing off her thick pretty legs.

"Now what can I do for you ladies?" he asked as he sipped from his wine glass.

"We're sorry to bother you Dreyfus, but as you know the fella's are away in Vegas, and Emerald City's low on supply," Yvette said.

"How is that? They just got over $500,000 worth of supply a few weeks ago. Are you telling me you're so low that you can't wait until they get back?"

"Yes I am. I'm sure you know that we run Emerald City. All they do is stop by to check the status. So we're the best people to tell you what's going on. Which is why I wanted to discuss something else with you," Yvette said just as smoothly as the wind blows. "We aren't in business with them anymore. So if you want in on the Emerald City business, you'll be dealin' with us from now on."

Dreyfus' laughter pissed me off but didn't faze Yvette. She didn't smile and didn't take her eyes off his the entire time.

"And just how do you intend on running an operation *alone*? I mean, you are some very beautiful ladies but I'm sure you know this business is a man's." He continued while chuckling.

"I'm sorry, Dreyfus, we were under the impression your only concern was cash. Not whether it was dealt from a man or a woman," I said.

"It is!" he said angrily. "But be careful pretty lady. Don't mistake my kindness for weakness. Now how do you know I'd even be interested in dealing with you? Man or woman?" he asked turning his attention back to Yvette.

"Because we're here to settle *their* bill, as well and pay you up front for the weight we need now," Yvette said as she stood up and placed the steel suitcase on the table covering his paper. She popped open suitcase containing over $500,000. Three hundred thousand was for the consignment and the rest was for what we needed now. When the case was open, she turned it toward him.

"Well I see you settled the bill, but there appears to be a little extra cash in here then what's owed," he said after seeing we were talking his language, *Dollar Bill*. "So what's the deal?"

"Like I said, we're settling their bill and paying up front. I realize that in the past you worked on a consignment basis for Emerald City. But going forward we're not going to operate like that. The interest we're paying is too high and the return is too low."

"Now why should I accept money upfront from you, when I can make almost thirty percent more on consignment with your little boyfriends?" He laughed. "This makes no fuckin' sense. You're not dealin' in the minor leagues, this is the majors!"

"You should accept our offer because if you don't, you'll be cut out of the Emerald City profit all together. Now I know you've become accustomed to your glamorous lifestyle," Yvette said as she turned around as if she was seeing his place for the first time. "I mean, your place is FAT. And I'm almost positive that Emerald City keeps you paid. I would hate to see you cut back a little," Yvette said slyly.

"You obviously didn't hear me little girl!" Dreyfus yelled becoming angry at the idea of a woman giving him options instead of the other way around. "Why the fuck should I fix somethin' that ain't broke? I'm fine with my current business arrangements. So unless you can tell me what *my* benefit is," he said as he removed stacks of money totaling $300 grand and closing the suitcase. "There ain't shit else to talk about."

"Did you know that the Emerald City squad is in Vegas right now meeting a new connect?"

When my friend gave up that morsel of information, the smile was completely wiped off Dreyfus's face.

She continued. "When they return, they have plans to settle the bill and sever *all* the ties with you. We don't want to do that. We love the product you provide and so do our customers. So what is your benefit? MONEY," Yvette said with a smile. She knew she knew from that point on she had his full attention.

"We want to pay up front because we've had several attempts on the houses. We don't want unpaid product to be fucked with. We rather give you what's owed up front, and handle business with whoever tries to fuck with us on the side. We don't want the two connecting anymore," I said.

I could tell we had got to him, and that the news of possibly losing income in Emerald City wasn't sitting well with him.

"Uh….do you know this for sure?" he asked more humbled in his approach. "I can't see them telling you so much of their business."

"They have two women with them now in Vegas, and one of our lieutenants has a relationship with her. Well…an understanding that is. And she advised him, and he told us," I said trying to seal the deal that Yvette was closing. "So do we have a deal?"

"You can wait if you'd like until they return to tell you the same thing. But if you do that, our deal is no longer open to you," Yvette said.

Damn! My girl was going in for the kill. He took off his glasses and stood up. As he walked toward the door, we got a good glimpse at how tall he was. He had to be about 6'4 and he was much more intimidating when standing. For a minute, I thought he was getting ready to blast our heads off. Instead, he closed the door and locked it behind him then made his way over to the couch against the wall and took a seat. As if he said something to Yvette I couldn't hear or understand, she stood up, removed her suit jacket which revealed the curves of her breasts, hips and legs. She slowly walked over to him, and knelt down.

Finally figuring out what was going on, I stood up from my chair and removed my suit jacket as well. He smiled as he saw my bare breasts with the diamond dropped necklace in between them. Unzipping my skirt, I slid out of it letting it fall to the floor revealing my white lace panties and pumps.

I moved toward the couch, cradling him with my breasts against his face. Yvette had already brought him to stiffness. And for a man in his late forties, he had it going on in the dick department for real. Tilting my head to the right so my soft curls could dress my shoulders and back, I kissed him on his lips tasting a hint of the wine he drank just moments earlier. I hadn't noticed that Yvette had already slid out of her skirt leaving nothing on but her black Jimmy Choo pumps and lace chemise. Working him to a complete thickness with her hand, she looked up at him and smiled at how his body shook as he anticipated her taking him into her mouth.

"Dreyfus," she started in a low, soft voice. "Do we have a deal?"

"Yes....." He moaned as she engulfed him fully while I fed him my nipples. "We have a deal."

I was surprised at the tongue skills he possessed on my breasts. I knew this was business but I had all intentions of taking advantage. Plus he was paid, and power always turned me on. He impressed me so much with his tongue action, that I was able to rearrange the setup to my advantage.

Yvette continued to suck his dick while I positioned my ass directly over his face. His pussy eating skills were as good as I'd hoped they'd be. He grabbed my ass while his tongue searched ferociously around my pussy devouring up all the months of built up tension. I was on the verge of cumming when I tried to pull away to give my girl enough time to do what she was doing. But as if he was starving, he placed his hands on my lower back pulling me closer toward his face. I had no other choice but to explode inside the mouth of a business associate and man I really didn't know. When I turned I saw Yvette was already done and dressed.

I got off him and quickly got dressed too. Yvette walked to his desk and wrote down her number. He smiled at both of us, and wiped my wetness off his mouth with a napkin. Tying his housecoat tightly, and putting his glasses back on, he told us when and where the weight would be delivered and to arrange for someone to unload it. We were almost out the door when he called us back.

"Ladies."

"Yes?" Yvette said holding the empty suitcase in her hand.

"I wasn't implying for you to go that far. I was sold the moment you told me they were using a new connect."

"I know," Yvette said, smiling.

"And you did it anyway?" he asked.

"Yeah.....I was tryin' to show you there are several benefits to working with a woman. And today you learned one of the most lucrative. Good night, Dreyfus. We'll be in contact," she said as we walked out the door.

"You's a bad bitch!" I laughed. "Do you even have a heart?!" I continued while we jumped in my Mercedes the valet pulled around front for us.

"Not anymore. Not anymore."

CHAPTER 28

THE TIME IS NOW
FEBRUARY, FRIDAY, 8:10 P.M.

DERRICK

The gatekeepers called a meeting in the community center around the back of Emerald City projects.

The meeting consisted of Doctanian, Derrick, Bruce, Jones, Harold and Ed. They called the meeting to let everybody know what was going on from here on out. Some people were happy about the change, because they didn't care for the Emerald City squad but some didn't.

"So what are we supposed to do when they ask us what's up with their cash?" Harold asked as he sat in his chair, balancing himself on the back two legs. "This doesn't make any sense."

"You're supposed to tell them to see us about it," Yvette responded, looking him dead in the eyes. "You can put full responsibility on us."

"You sure 'bout that." He laughed as he looked at Ed.

"I'm positive," she snapped. "But can you handle what we're asking you to do?"

"Hey.....as long as I get my cash, I ain't trippin'." He laughed as he gave Ed dap.

"So why you ask?" Yvette shot back not liking his response.

"Huh?" Harold said.

"I said, if you were totally comfortable, all that shit you asked me before was a waste of fuckin' time," she said making him feel stupid.

"Does anybody else have any *legitimate* questions?" Mercedes added, in an attempt to help Yvette gain control over the meeting.

"I do," Derrick asked, sizing Mercedes up in her black fitted pants and black button down top.

"Go ahead, Derrick," Mercedes said.

"Are ya'll good on manpower? I can give up two more of my boys if the ones you have on my squad ain't enough."

"Naw, we good. Thanks," she said giving him a look that lingered on longer than it should have. It was clear that they were feeling each other up.

"Well if nobody else has any other questions, the meeting is adjourned. I'm expectin' them to come through tomorrow night. Be on guard. If you see anything suspicious, hit us on the Blackberry," Yvette added.

As the lieutenants made their way to the door, Yvette called Doctanian and Derrick back. When she was sure the others were out of sight, she addressed them.

"Listen....I'm gonna need ya'll to be lookin' out for Harold and Ed. I have a feelin' they gonna do us greasy," Yvette whispered.

"I was thinkin' the same thing," Derrick said.

"And you know whatever I can do I'm in," Doctanian added.

"Thanks. Have you heard anything 'bout Jordan yet?" Mercedes asked Doctanian.

Everything about him had changed since Jordan had gone missing. He didn't take care of his appearance the way he use to. He let himself go and wasn't sociable. The biggest indicator that he wasn't the same came from L'il C. He kept coming to her saying something was wrong with Doctanian. She was afraid her son had gotten to attached to a man who owed him nothing. It was also the first time she'd ever seen her son worried.

"No. I ain't heard nothin'. I'm tellin' you, if somebody hurt her I'ma kill 'em!" he said, fighting back tears.

"I understand. And if *you* need us to do anything, let me know."

"And if I hear anything, I'm puttin' it to anybody who got anything to do with it!" Derrick said. "That's my word."

"Thanks man! She's pregnant wit' my kid!" he said forcing back tears.

Yvette and Mercedes liked Doctanian. He was a real man who was true to the game and didn't deserve the hand he was being dealt. But at the same time they had a business to run. The question now was did they keep him on and jeopardize the organization or fire him which would ultimately be a slap in the face.

"Take it easy Doctanian, we'll talk to you later," Yvette said.

"Thanks." He walked out the door.

As he walked out the three of them were left alone.

"Derrick, keep an eye on him. I'm worried about him," Yvette said.

"Done," Derrick said.

CHAPTER 29
SOMETHIN' AIN'T RIGHT
FEBRUARY, MONDAY, 7:10 P.M.

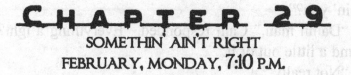

"I'm telling you them bitches are up to somethin'! Why can't we get through to nobody at EC?!" Thick yelled as he drove to Emerald City.

"Calm down man. Sometimes you blow shit outta proportion!" Cam wasn't feeling how Thick was acting anymore. The truth was, after the stunt he pulled in the hotel with bringing them the girls, and then keeping them in his room the whole time pissed him off. It wasn't because he liked them or anything, but it was the principle. He didn't even ask Cam if he could slide off with the shorty who was supposed to be for him. That's just the type of grimy ass nigga he had become.

"Yeah man you wildin' out now. We on our way now. We'll see what the deal is," Lavelle added. "No need to get worked up yet."

"I know one thing, if Yvette fuckin' wit' me, I'm puttin' my hands around her throat."

While on the way to EC, Cam's cell phone rang. He smiled when he saw it was L'il C's cell phone. He hadn't spoken to him since he returned from Vegas. He missed him and his mother but he couldn't express how much he missed her. He had to keep it real with L'il C about his and Mercedes' relationship, and right now they were over.

"Hey man!" Cam yelled into the phone.

"Hey dad." L'il C wasn't his usual upbeat self. "When I'm seein' you?"

"Damn man," Cam responded. "Everything a'ight? You sound a little out of it."

"Not really."

Thick started blasting the music in the truck. Cam was trying to talk to his son and Thick was acting stupid. Cam had to be careful in his approach. Number one it was wrong to tell a man to adjust the volume in his own truck, and number two Thick was a hot head. Saying the wrong thing could almost guarantee an argument. But he was going to turn the music down whether he wanted to or not.

"Hey man...you mind turnin' that shit down?" Cam asked.

"Actually I do."

Lavelle and Dyson were pissed about his response. L'il C was like their nephew and couldn't believe how Thick was acting.

"Come on man...turn that shit down so the man can talk to his son!" Lavelle yelled over the music.

Thick looked at Cameron through the mirror and Cam stared him dead in the eyes.

"Aw come on. Cam don't know when a nigga playin' wit' him?" He joked as he adjusted the volume. "Ya'll niggas been blowin' me all weekend actin' all serious and shit. Tell L'il C I said what up."

Cameron ignored any him. He couldn't believe how he'd been acting ever since Dex was killed. He couldn't stand him and was starting to even hate him.

"Dad...is everything okay?" L'il C questioned.

For a second Cam was so caught up in his anger that he

didn't hear his son.

"Dad. You there?"

"Oh…Yeah. I didn't hear you at first l'il man. But what's goin' on with you?"

"They can't find Jordan…and Doc don't hang wit' me no more. It's like he don't even know me."

Cam was listening to his son but also peeped how Thick kept eyeing him through the rearview mirror and wondered what was up with that.

"What you mean they can't find Jordan?" Cam didn't know a lot about her but he did know she was Doctanian's girl.

"They don't know where she at. Mamma says they been lookin' but I think somebody got her."

"Don't worry about stuff like that L'il C. Leave the worryin' to me."

"O.K."

"Where you at?" Cam asked positive that more drama was going on in Emerald City than he thought.

"I'm at cousin Vickie's in Virginia."

"Cousin Vickie's? Is Chante and the baby wit' you too?" Cam knew it was weird for them to be over there because Mercedes couldn't stand Vickie. I mean, she knew she would do right by the kids, but as much as Mercedes hated her guts, he couldn't help but wonder how she ended up smoothing things out enough to drop their children off.

"Yep. We all over here. She says we gonna be here till it all blows over."

"Till what blows over?" Cam asked wondering how much L'il C really knew.

"She calls it the 'Showdown'."

Cam was quiet. *The Show Down?* He thought. *What in the fuck is this bitch up to?*

"Listen L'il C," he said. "Doc will be okay. I'll holla at him when I get back to EC."

"For real? That's what's up!"

"Yeah, don't worry about it."

"He said we were gonna start a music company together. He said if I stopped selling drugs, we'd be like Dame Dash and Jay Z!"

"WHAT!" Cam yelled taking in what he just heard. He yelled so loud everybody turned around to ear hustle in on what he was saying to L'il C. "What you talkin' 'bout man? What do you mean he stopped you from selling drugs."

"Yeah." He hesitated. "It's okay now. I'm not doin' it anymore."

Cam was listening but all he was thinking about was which one of them niggas put him on. I mean, he knew it was just a matter of time before L'il C got into the life but he imagined it would be when he was older. *I'm gonna kill whoever the fuck disrespected me! That's my word!* He thought.

"You alright man?" Thick asked.

"I'm good."

"L'il C," he said real low. "Who gave you weight to sell? And tell me the truth."

L'il C paused. "Uncle Thick dad."

CHAPTER 30

TOO LITTLE TOO LATE
FEBRUARY, MONDAY, 9:30 P.M.

DOCTANIAN

"Are you sure?! Don't play wit' me!" Doctanian told one of the heads.

"Yeah I'm sure. I saw him meet her 'round back and then dump her body later," he said, anticipating the reward Doctanian would give him for the news.

Doctanian's body was shaking with anger. He couldn't believe he'd lost the love of his life at the hands of his most trusted soldier.

"Doc! Look at your leg!"

When he looked down, he saw piss streaming down the jeans he'd worn for the past few days. Ever since he'd been trying to find Jordan, he'd been an emotional wreck. He didn't take care of his body. He didn't eat. And most of all, he didn't care for anything or anybody.

Without saying a word, he walked off. He was too angry to be embarrassed or even cold that he was walking in his own piss. He hadn't had an episode like that since he was a kid. When he was younger, whenever he was afraid or upset, he would piss in his bed. It went on for years because his father would beat his mother and he'd stay awake at night feeling defenseless and helpless. It didn't stop until he and his

171

mother moved to Emerald City together.

"Hey!" the dope fiend yelled. "What 'bout my stuff?"

Doctanian turned around and the fiend rushed over to him. He handed him everything he had in his pockets. He was sure he'd spend all night getting high but he didn't care.

Because in his mind, tonight would be his last night alive.

CHAPTER 31
HOLLA AT YOU
FEBRUARY, MONDAY, 9:40 P.M.

DOCTANIAN

"Let me holla at you for a second man," Doctanian said with a glazed look in his eye.

"Naw Joe. I got somewhere to go right now," Erick responded holding onto the weapon in his pocket.

He wasn't a fool. He saw the crazed look in his eyes and he knew what the deal was. Doctanian had been walking around like a mummy ever since he dumped Jordan's lifeless body into a dumpster.

"Why man? Any other time you got conversation for me. Why not now?"

They were in the same alley where CJ and Charles were killed. Their bodies were pumping adrenaline as they realized, somebody wouldn't be leaving the alley alive.

"She was a whore! I had to do it," Erick said, feeling there was no need in wasting time or lying. He decided to get the shit out in the open. "You gonna end what we got over a whore? Think about what we could have man. Let's take down these bitches and make shit happen! I talked to Ed and Harold and they ready to take them bitches out tonight! What's up? Let's put this shit to the side man!"

Tears rolled down his face as he focused on Erick. He

knew he was only talking to throw him off. The moment he let his guard down, Erick's gun would be in his back.

"Why you hurt Jordan? You knew she was all I had?" Doctanian asked, searching for answers that he knew Erick didn't have.

"Are you serious?" Erick laughed taking his gun out of his pocket. "I'm telling you we got a chance at a dynasty and you worried about a bitch and a baby that probably wasn't even yours?" He laughed. "Are you really that soft?"

His words stabbed him in the heart.

"Are you telling me you fucked my girl?" He took two steps toward him.

"That's exactly what I'm saying. And I fucked her well."

With that, Doctanian took his gun out and without the slightest hesitation, pulled the trigger. But as if he was in a bad movie, nothing came out.

"Oh snap! This really is my lucky day!" Erick laughed relieved he wasn't shot. "But it ain't yours," he said.

Erick aimed his weapon but dropped to his knees before he could get a shot off. Doctanian watched in amazement as a round of bullets found a home inside his back. His knees hit the ground first as he looked at Doctanian, and then fell to the concrete face down, revealing who was behind him.

Derrick kept his promise to the girls and looked after Doctanian after all.

Instead of feeling relief, Doctanian ran to pick up Derrick's gun and placed it in his mouth. Derrick rushed him taking it away.

"What in the fuck is wrong wit' you man!" Why you doin' this?!"

"Cuz I don't deserve to live!" He cried.

"Come on man! He's dead. We killed his ass for Jordan."

"No...I don't deserve to live because it was my fault

Jordan was murdered."

"Why you say that?" Derrick asked.

"Because he was punishing me for killing Stacia and Dex."

CHAPTER 32

GET AT ME
FEBRUARY, MONDAY, 10:15 P.M.

THICK

"Hey man, open the gate! What the fuck you waitin' on?!" Thick yelled.

"I'm sorry Thick. I have to phone Yvette first"

"The fuck you mean you have to phone Yvette?!"

Thick was growing irritated at the way the guard was treating him. In the past, the moment any of the guards saw his truck they'd fling open the gate to Emerald City. But here he was acting as if Thick was a customer and didn't deserve the VIP treatment he was accustomed to.

"Yall hear this shit man?" he said as he looked back at Cameron and them. "Them bitches really askin' for it! This is what the fuck I was talkin' about."

"Well we're here now," Cameron responded still salty at what L'il C told him about Thick giving him dope to sell. "We'll see what's up."

When the time was right, Cameron would step to Thick about the situation.

Lavelle and Dyson were quiet as they waited on the word from the guard. They were mentally preparing for what they would have to do, and what they knew Thick wanted to do. There wasn't a doubt in any of their minds that tonight, somebody would die.

It was just a matter of who.

"Okay sir!" The guard said. "You can go through now." The gate rose.

"The next time you see me…you gonna wish you didn't pull this shit," Thick promised. "Don't let them bitches fill your head. I run…I mean…we run shit in Emerald City." He corrected himself, realizing his own selfish motives almost slipped out.

The guard didn't say anything. He knew he had to stick to the orders Yvette and them gave him. They treated him better than Thick ever did.

Pulling up in front of Unit C, they noticed the women weren't on post. Thick got cocky when he saw that. He immediately started thinking that they must've been frightened after the shit they pulled at the gate and were hiding out. But the others knew better. They realized something more was going on and everything was changing tonight.

"Derrick…get down here!" Thick yelled as they all jumped out of the truck.

Derrick moved slowly. He no longer showed urgency the way they were used to seeing. Thick, Cameron, Lavelle and Dyson noticed that their authority was diminished.

"Yeah…what you need?" Derrick asked nonchalantly.

"What I need? What I need?! Who the fuck you talkin' to like that nigga?!" Thick shot back as he walked up on Derrick. "You got a death wish son?"

Derrick took two steps back, brushed off his coat and said, "Like I said…what you need?"

When Cameron saw Thick was getting ready to pull his gun out of his coat and kill Derrick, he stepped up to him. Five of Derrick's soldiers hurried to Derrick's side. When Lavelle and Dyson saw that, they all rushed to Thick's side too. Right or wrong, they weren't tolerating disrespect from somebody that was under them.

"I know you ain't crazy, D!" Lavelle said. "So you betta start telling us what the fuck is up."

"I asked a question I still ain't get an answer to. What do ya'll need?" Derrick was unmoved by them. "Ya'll here to cop some dope or what?" His soldiers were on point to blast the squad's heads off and if they missed, they had ten other soldiers hidden from view with sniper weapons ready to snub them out.

Thick was stuck motionless and speechless. In all his life he always provoked fear but tonight was different.

"Where Yvette and them?" Dyson asked taking control of the situation.

"I'll take ya'll to 'em." Derrick said.

"Yeah…we need to find out what the fuck is goin' on 'round here," Cameron demanded.

While the others talked, Thick's eyes stayed glued on Derrick. Any other day he would've killed him where he stood, but this time was different. He was walking into a situation blind and he wanted to be cool and get some answers first. But he also wanted Derrick to know that he wouldn't forget his disrespect and would be handling him later.

Derrick sensing the hate in his eyes said, "I feel the same way playa."

Silence.

"Yo Doc…come around and pick us up around front. We takin' Thick and them to the girls," Derrick spoke into his walkie-talkie.

"You got it man."

When Thick heard Doctanian's voice he developed a plan.

Five minutes later Doctanian pulled up in a White Ford Excursion. Derrick jumped in the passenger seat and the other soldiers hoped in the back. Before they pulled off, Thick asked to speak to Doc in private.

"You want us to go with you?" Lavelle asked.

"Naw…go wait in the truck.

Doc hopped out of the driver's seat and they walked together. Thick was going to do his best to play on his emotions. But what Thick didn't know was that Jordan was already dead and he didn't have anything or anybody else to lose.

"Listen…I need you to do me a favor," Thick said to Doctanian with his hand on his back. His mouth hidden from view so that no one could read his lips but Doc.

"And what's that?"

"I need you to take out Derrick and possibly Yvette and them bitches."

Doctanian turned to him and said, "Sorry youngin'…I can't do nothin' for you."

Thick couldn't believe what was going on. He was the most ruthless out of the group and everyone was carrying the utmost fuck out of him tonight. *What are these bitches doin'? Fuckin these dudes?* He thought.

"Oh for real? I wonder if you would feel the same way if I paid a little visit to your girl." He threatened.

Doctanian wasn't moved. He had already lost Jordan and Yvette and the girls were the only family he had. It was through blackmailing that he was able to get him to kill Dex and Stacia. Thick told him he would gut out his pregnant girlfriend and maybe even his mother. So with no more convincing needed, he did what he was told. The look in Dex and Stacia's eyes still fucked with him till this day. Instead of being scared when he popped up out of nowhere requesting a ride to the ball, they smiled. Not knowing that he was there to kill them. But it was Thick who decided to slice their bodies, and Doctanian hated him for that. Almost as much as he hated not being man enough to stand up to Thick. But tonight, all that had changed.

Telling Derrick everything lifted a major weight off his shoulders. He didn't even tell Jordan about his hand in Stacia and Dex's murder because he didn't want to get her involved.

"I don't know what she'll say man...she's dead," he said as he walked back to the truck and jumped in leaving Thick standing alone looking stupid.

"You comin' or not?" Doctanian asked from the driver side of the truck.

Thick decided to bite his words but now he had added Doctanian to his list along with his mother. And since he liked L'il C so much, he was gonna take him out too.

Thick jumped in his truck and pulled up alongside theirs. "Where we goin?"

"To the community center," Derrick said as Doctanian started the truck. "Follow us."

"Hold up right quick," Thick said when his phone vibrated.

He was shocked to see who it was. Yvette was calling him. He laughed and before he answered, he showed the squad members the caller ID.

"You can't be serious!" Lavelle said.

"Answer it," Cameron added. "Maybe we can find out what the fuck is going on."

"Hello."

"Thick...I see you out front. Why don't you come upstairs and talk to me for a second," Yvette said as if they were still together. "I got something I want to give to you."

"Oh really?" He laughed.

"Yes...and your key still works," she said as he hung up.

When he hung up, he noticed Derrick and them still looking at him.

"You rollin' or what man?" Derrick asked.

"Naw…Cameron and them going. I got something else to take care of now."

He told his friends that Yvette wanted to see him and that he may have to choke her.

"You sure you don't want us comin' with you?" Lavelle asked. "This seems like a set up."

"Nigga please. I'm time enough for a bitch. She not crazy enough to fuck wit me," he said jumping out of the truck. "You drive Cam!"

Cameron got in the front seat. Thick waved them off and went into the building.

He had one thing on his mind and that was putting Yvette in her place.

CHAPTER 33
FULL CIRCLE
FEBRUARY, MONDAY, 10:45 P.M.

THICK

Walking up to the door felt eerie for Thick.

But being the arrogant, cocky man he was he pushed his feelings to the side and walked into the apartment he once shared with Yvette as if they still lived their...*together.* What he saw next he couldn't deny. Everything in the apartment was gone. It looked the same way it did when they first moved in.

With the door still open and his hand tucked in his coat for his piece, he walked in. With the door slightly ajar, he used the light in the hallway to help him see. The only thing in the apartment was two chairs in the middle of the floor. He tried to flip the switch for the lights but they didn't come on. He saw Yvette sitting in one of the chairs as she lit two candles.

Again, Thick flipped the switch as if flipping it the first ten times were a fluke.

"Thick...it's not on. Come in and have a seat.

The chair Yvette was sitting in was directly across from the empty one. When Thick closed the door, the light from the candle revealed her sexy small frame. He couldn't help but admire how good she looked. She was wearing all black and had her hair combed down her back. The tight black pants she had on made her legs look even more appealing. The button down shirt she had on kissed her cleavage perfectly as the diamonds she had in her earrings and on her neck illuminated the way.

Thick walked in and took his seat. The candle in the middle of the chairs cast a glow on both their faces.

"What's up, Yvette? I'm here. You got somebody in here for me or somethin'? Cause if you do bring it on."

"Nobody's here Thick."

He went through the apartment to inspect himself and found she was telling the truth.

"You see?" Yvette smiled. "It's just you and me."

Her glossy lips answered his questions elegantly. Yvette didn't appear nervous and her mannerisms put Thick on edge.

"Well what the fuck is up then?!" he asked taking his seat again.

"You were always a man who liked to get to the point."

"Yep…and shit ain't changed so stop wasting my muthafuckin time!"

"Shit ain't changed, Thick?" She laughed. "Shit ain't changed? A lot of shit has changed."

"Oh yeah…like what?"

"For starters you ruined my life and left me to pick up the pieces by myself."

"Is that what this is about?" He laughed again, his deep voice rocking the empty apartment. "Damn bitch! I thought you'd be over big "T" by now."

"I wanna know why?" She was unmoved by his comments.

"Why I do what? Stop fuckin' wit' you?"

"Yes."

"Cuz you're weak! That's why."

"I hold shit down for you and you call me weak? I wonder how many other women could hold shit down for their men."

"You probably right. But you wanted to do it. That's why it was so easy for you to hold shit down."

"Is that what you think, Thick?" She crossed her legs. "Do you really believe I wanted to be a hustler, riskin' my life everyday?"

"I know you did."

"Well you're wrong. I wanted you, but you chose another bitch over me. You gave her my life and left me wit' nothin'. I would've done anything for you, Thick. Anything you asked me."

"I know. That's the problem." He laughed. "You didn't have limits, and she wasn't that way. Plus she took a scar for me."

"So she gets in a car accident...and get's a scar on her face, and wins points with you? Are you serious?"

"Yeah...I am."

When he said that, Yvette reached under her leg and pulled out a pearl handled knife. Thick sat up in his seat and pulled out his gun.

"She gets a scar and you chose her huh?" With that said, she took the knife and sliced along her jaw line. As the blood trickled down, she never took her eyes off his. "I bet you she wouldn't have done that shit."

Thick looked at her and suddenly he was turned on. Yvette was more thorough then he thought. She reminded him of the old Yvette he dated but better.

"You a crazy bitch. But I like that shit!"

"I'm glad you do. Now on to business. Your services are no longer needed in Emerald City. We're takin' over."

"FUCK you talkin' 'bout, Yvette? You sound stupid!" His voiced boomed through the empty apartment.

She sat firm in her chair, not fazed. "I'm talkin' 'bout how you gonna die tonight."

Thick wasn't laughing anymore. He thought after her cutting her face she'd beg to be back with him. But here she was threatening to kill him.

"Yeah okay. And just how you supposed to do that."

"Like this," she said as she pitched the knife through the air burying it into his neck.

She stood up and walked toward him. The same slick, manipulative eyes she'd become accustomed to were two sizes larger than usual. He tried desperately to get the knife out of his neck but couldn't move. Standing behind him, she whispered in his ear.

"You see baby. Some promises. You gotta keep."

When his big body slid out of the chair and onto the floor, she grabbed her coat and moved toward the door.

185

CHAPTER 34

A ROOM
FEBRUARY, MONDAY, 10:45 P.M.

I did what the fuck I had to do!

I gave him my life. My fucking life! And what does he do, act like he can't remember it. Killing him was as easy as getting my pussy ate. That's right…it felt so good I could've came. I didn't choose this life it chose me. And I accepted it…for him.

When I opened up the door to the community center, I was happy to see Cameron, Lavelle and Dyson were there. Kenyetta, Carrissa and Mercedes were there also. I could tell by the look in the men's eyes that they were scared when I appeared without Thick.

My girls were wondering what happened to my face and I motioned to them with my eyes that everything was okay.

"Hello gentlemen," I said not explaining Thick's absence or my fresh scar. "How are you doin' tonight."

"Stop playin' games, Yvette. What the fuck is goin' on?" Lavelle said.

"Please…have a seat." I told them.

As they took their seats around the table in the meeting room in the community center, I was trying to be careful. I had a big decision to make tonight. You would've thought the biggest decision I had to make was killing Thick. But that was easy and necessary. He would've never relinquished Emerald City to us.

When they all had a seat, and Derrick, Doctanian and the other soldiers remained standing surrounding the table, I sat down across from them. Mercedes, Kenyetta and Carissa sat down next to me. I could see the love they had for them, but I could also feel the loyalty they had to me. Besides, we all had been lied to and betrayed and as far as I was concerned, we were no longer loyal to them.

"I'm not gonna beat 'round the bush wit' you...we takin' over Emerald City," I said looking into all of their eyes.

"This bitch is delusional!" Cameron laughed. "How the fuck you gonna run Emerald City alone?"

"Easy." Mercedes added. "Have you forgotten who's been runnin' shit anyway?"

"You've been runnin' shit wit' our help," Lavelle responded.

"Actually I don't think we'll notice the difference. You haven't had our backs in a while," Carissa said.

"First off...you don't have a relationship with Dreyfus. He don't fuck wit' females like that so your supply would be cut the fuck off," Dyson added.

We all started laughing makin' them even more anxious. After all, we were telling them how their futures would turn out and there wasn't a damn thing they could do about it.

"Yeah...Dreyfus is somethin' else isn't he?" I said.

"Yes he is...and he doesn't work wit' females," Cameron added.

"Maybe...maybe not," I told him. "All I know is he has a bad ass house. I'm telling you the waterfall was outrageous. What did you think, Mercedes?"

"I don't know, Yvette," she said as she shrugged her

shoulders. "I liked his head better. He can suck a mean pussy."

Cameron's face went red out of anger. "Oh so you fuckin' Dreyfus now?"

"Sit down playa," Derrick said. "Slow your roll."

Cameron looked up at him and sat back down.

"And where are my fucking kids while you out tossing pussy at that nigga? Huh? Where my kids?"

Mercedes laughed. "Don't' worry baby...they weren't there."

Cameron wanted to smack the shit out of Mercedes but Lavelle pulled him back down.

"What makes you think we'd just walk away from a million dollar empire?"

"For one we've doubled the salary of our soldiers so they have our backs, and Dreyfus doesn't want to fuck wit' you for your betrayal in Vegas," I told them.

"Ya'll told him about that?" Dyson asked.

"Of course!" Kenyetta laughed.

"And how did ya'll know?" Cameron added.

"Let's just say ya'll should choose the female company ya'll take with you on business trips more wisely in the future." I advised.

Lavelle shook his head in disgust.

"So ya'll have a connection wit' Dreyfus and now we're out huh? Well what about the money we put in this shit? We ain't walkin' away empty handed," Dyson said.

With that, I snapped my fingers and one of the soldiers placed a steel suitcase on the table. I popped the latches, looked at the money, and turned it around to them.

"It's all there." I assured them sliding the case across the table.

They looked at each other, visibly shook.

"Well what'll happen if we don't buy this shit?" Cameron said.

"Then you'll end up like Thick," I said.

"And how's that?" Lavelle asked.

I looked around the table. "Dead."

They jumped up from their seats and pulled out weapons as our soldiers placed three barrels to their heads apiece.

"Don't make this nastier then it has to be. You did us wrong and you know it, and now it's time to step down," I said. "Either way somebody loses but don't forget about the kids involved. If you don't step down, somebody will get killed because we won't stop fighting until the last breath leaves our bodies. And that could mean L'il C without a mother or father. Or what about Lavelle's kids? Everybody loses if these guns pop in here tonight."

"Ya'll have other shops. Ya'll don't need EC," Carissa said.

The look on their faces was that of defeat, remorse and guilt. They knew they had did us wrong and we deserved Emerald City. No fuck that, we earned it! They also knew if they didn't step down, we were fully prepared for war.

"So what's up? Do you step down or not?" I said.

They looked at each other and grabbed the money off the table without saying a word.

"That was a good decision," Yvette said. "Now can you do us one more solid?"

"And what the fuck is that Yvette?" Cameron responded still not believing everything that took place. "Take your dead friend with you? He's up in my apartment."

CHAPTER 35
THE CONFRONTATION
FEBRUARY, MONDAY, 10:45 P.M.

EMERALD CITY

Cameron and them were twisted up a little about how things went down.

Part of them wanted to do more, but they had them out-numbered. It was obvious that any of the soldiers would've gave their lives for the girls no questions asked.

Cameron, Lavelle and Dyson eased into Yvette's apartment. They were met by the smell of blood and fear as soon as they opened the door. However, it wasn't the smell of death floating in the air that made them grab for their weapons. It was the movement.

"Help...me," Thick said, barely above a whisper. "Help me."

They all rushed to his side with the light from the candle leading them.

"We thought you were dead man!" Lavelle yelled.

"We'll get you out of here," Dyson added.

They were helpful but Cameron wasn't. The thought of all the trouble Thick had caused consumed him. All this shit was Thick's greedy ass fault. Had he not brought Zakayla into the picture, he would be marrying Mercedes and business would have been as usual. He looked at Dyson and Lavelle and as if they could read his mind Dyson said, "Make it quick."

"We'll be in the hallway," Lavelle added taking one last look at Thick, the man he once called friend.

Cameron stooped down in front of Thick who was moving on the floor trying to hang on to life.

"Help me. Please."

"I want my face to be the last face you see."

"Cam...get me outta here," he begged. "I'm dying nigga!"

"I'm sorry dawg. I can't do shit for you."

Thick dragged his bloody body along the floor and tried to appeal to Cameron.

"Why man? Why...why, are you doing this to me?"

"Because you fucked with the wrong nigga's son," Cameron said as he placed his gun to his head. "And now you know."

He pulled his trigger and blasted the bullet into Thick's skull. Once the shot was heard Lavelle and Dyson came back in the apartment.

"Well...let's get rid of this muthafucka," Lavelle said.

"Yeah, let's get rid of him."

~~EPILOGUE~~

2 YEARS LATER

Life in Emerald City was different.

The gatekeepers didn't have to hold down the gate anymore. They all moved back to the steps of Emerald City three times out of the week and empowered their soldiers to do the work. They made decisions to enjoy life with the people in their lives that meant the most…their family and each other.

Mercedes got with Derrick and had another baby. They bought a house in Upper Marlboro, Maryland. Derrick was still holding shit down in Emerald City with his crew and he realized that reporting to a woman wasn't as bad as he thought.

Carissa got back with Lavelle but tried to do it on the DL. She would sneak off to see him and when Yvette let on that she knew, Carissa said she feared that they would reject her. But they all knew that Lavelle really loved her and no matter what, they at least deserved a chance.

Kenyetta started keeping time with one of the Tyland Towers dudes. Nobody knew who he was and nobody asked too many questions either. She said when he was worth introducing she'd bring him around but not a minute sooner.

Yvette didn't mess with anybody anymore. Everybody swore she was keeping time with a female, some chick named Spinner, but she denied it. The more she denied it the more they felt she was lying up with her. But just like they accepted Carissa and Lavelle, they would accept Yvette because no matter what they loved her.

Cameron had a hard time of letting Mercedes go. He did everything from coming by her and Derrick's house all hours of the night asking about the whereabouts of his kids, to showing up at places they were starting trouble. When none of that worked, he finally confessed his love to Mercedes but she said she was in love with Derrick. And when he saw it in her eyes, he left it alone.

One of Dyson's soldiers at one of his shops outside of Emerald rob and killed him. His body was never found and to this day Cameron and them are looking for whoever killed him.

Doctanian left the game and opened a sports bar. He moved his mother out of the projects and kept money stashed to keep his promise to L'il C about starting their video production company. He had a baby with a girl he met at his bar and was very happy.

Emerald City was built on fear and ran by lies but was uplifted by fearless women who called the men in their lives out.

And although they broke their promises, the women were better for it.

Cameron had a hard time of letting Mercedes go. He did everything from coming by her and Derrick's house all hours of the night asking about the whereabouts of his kids, to showing up at places they were starting trouble. When none of that worked, he finally confessed his love to Mercedes but she said she was in love with Derrick. And when he saw it in her eyes, he left it alone.

FUCK A HAPPILY EVER AFTER! THIS A MUTHAFUCKIN HOOD TALE! NOW LET ME SHOW YOU HOW SHIT REALLY WENT DOWN.

And although they broke their promises, the women were better for it.

Now The Drama Really Begins

DECEMBER 13TH, MONDAY, 9:33 P.M.

CAMERON

Cameron sat outside in his black 750i BMW without the heat running in the car.

It was thirty degrees outside and the wind was mighty. Despite the weather, his body was pumping fire due to what he was about to do. As hard as he tried, he couldn't get over losing Mercedes despite the break-up being all his fault. He felt betrayed and it caused him to mastermind the ultimate plan. When he saw Black Water walk toward his car, he hit the automatic unlock button. Black Water opened the car door and climbed in the passenger seat wearing a thick red North Face coat.

They called him Black Water because his complexion was dark and whether it was cold or hot outside, his skin kept its oily luster. Snow from the outside fell onto the butter colored leather seat. His build was as large as Thick's was and in a way, he reminded Cameron of him. That was another reason why he had trouble trusting him, but he pushed the thought out his mind because he was blinded by fury.

"Why you ain't got the heat on man? It's cold as shit in

195

here!" Black Water said, reaching over and hitting the button releasing a soft blast of warm air into the car.

Cameron mugged him wanting to give him a piece of his mind for touching the controls in his car. The only reason he didn't was because he needed his help. He had a lot of power in Tyland Towers so he'd come in handy for what he wanted done.

"I ain't ask you out here to make you comfortable. This is about business," Cameron said, his eyes hidden under the black New York Yankees cap he wore.

"So what *do* you want?"

"I want you to help me get Emerald back," Cameron said coldly.

"Get Emerald back?" Black Water chuckled. "I heard you niggas handed it over. Why you want it back now?"

The fact that everyone talked about how the Emerald City squad stepped down for some women bugged the hell out of him.

"Yeah well you shouldn't believe everything you hear. I was gettin' enough money to keep me tight but now I want more." He was lying. Cameron was still well off with his shops in and around D.C. His real reason for the betrayal of his children's mother was jealousy.

"You got people who can help me get in? I hear them shorties got that thing on lock over there."

"Yeah. My man Harold and Ed still there and they waitin' on my word. You shouldn't have a problem breakin' shit down, wit' my help. We just gonna have to be slow and careful."

"Cool," he said satisfied with his response. "So when you wanna start?"

"Today."

"And what about her?"

Cameron was silent. He knew once he gave the word, he couldn't change his mind later. He had to be clear on his intentions for Mercedes.

"Kill her."

PITBULLS IN A SKIRT 2

THE FINALE

COMING SOON

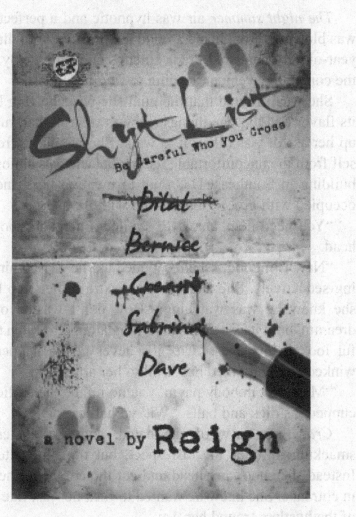

"Shyt List" The Novel Excerpt

CHAPTER ONE

HOOD LOVE AT ITS BEST

The night summer air was hypnotic and a perfect breeze was blowing through and around the inner city buildings. 19-year-old Yvonna's red Prada stilettos clicked quickly against the concrete pavement, leading toward her block.

She was irritated that the gum she was chewing had lost its flavor and that the thongs she was wearing had run so far up her ass, it was difficult to walk. She would've freed herself from the uncomfortable feeling but she was almost at her building in Southeast D.C. Not to mention her hands were occupied with grocery bags filled with food.

"You need help, shawty?!" yelled a neighborhood block head.

"Naw I'm good," she responded as she passed him walking seductively. She added a little extra in her step because she knew he was watching. "Boy, don't waste your time dreamin' bout it," she paused turning around to catch the lustful look in his eyes. "Cuz it's never gonna happen." She winked and continued her stroll to her apartment.

"Man ain't nobody payin' you no mind," he replied as he cupped his dick and balls. "Wit' yo half crazy ass."

Crazy was a word she hated, and she contemplated smacking him for the disrespect, but thought better of it. Instead she shook her head and cut the corner of the fenced in entrance. She knew he wanted to fuck her just like the rest of the hustlers 'round her way.

As her mind wondered, she thought about Cream, one of her best girlfriends. She was mad at her for dropping her off two blocks from her building. If Cream hadn't fucked Yvonna's neighbor's husband, she would've been able to drop her off out front.

But Treyana swore that if she saw her anywhere near her block she'd stomp a mud hole in her ass. And with six brothers and sisters, Cream knew Treyana meant it. She didn't stop at just fucking him, she went as far as to shack up in a run down motel off of New York Avenue in D.C. with his bum ass. Best believe the dogs were called out on her, so Cream hid out.

When Yvonna reached the apartment building she shared with her 6 year old sister and as she would say, her senile veteran father, she managed to free three fingers to grab the building's door. Once inside she cracked it open, stuck her foot in to hold it steady and twirled her body inside. The glass door bounced on her ass once before she took two steps forward and allowed it to close fully behind her. She briefly placed the bags on the floor to catch her breath and looked up at the two flights of stairs she had to tackle before *finally* getting some rest.

"Damn! Maybe I should've let his ass help!" she said out loud.

Picking the bags back up, she forced herself up the dimly lit hallway. She smiled when she saw her door realizing in a minute she'd be able to get naked, sit on the couch and munch on the oatmeal crème pies she had in one of the bags.

Now upstairs, Yvonna placed the bags on the floor and reached for the keys in her pocket. Before letting herself in, she dug in her ass and adjusted the thong that had been holding her hostage for the past few minutes. She was so caught up in bullshit, that she hadn't heard or sensed the person in the dark hallway behind her.

"Don't scream," he whispered heavily in her ear as he placed his left hand firmly against her mouth. She could smell the faint scent of cocoa butter since his index finger was directly under her nose. "You fuckin' hear me?"

She nodded her head yes.

"Open the door."

It took her a minute to find the right key on the Burberry

keychain. The sound of them jingling resonated in the hallway. When she located the key, she did as instructed and allowed him in as she wrestled with the bags.

"Hurry the fuck up!" he whispered again.

With the bags against the living room wall, they walked in and he locked the door behind them.

The apartment was totally dark with the exception of the light which illuminated from the huge fish tank against the living room wall. Just as she expected, her 6 year old sister Jesse was asleep and she saw no signs of her father.

With his hand still over her mouth he mumbled, "Now walk over to the couch! You betta not scream. You hear me?!"

She nodded yes. When she reached the couch, she bent over the edge as he demanded. With her ass in the air and her knees slightly bent, he reveled at her sexiness. The red Baby Phat shorts looked as if they were painted on. Still, they were in the way for what he had planned. With that, he tugged at them until they hung loosely at her ankles.

"Dayyyuummm!" he said focusing on her honey brown ass in the purple thongs. Then he ripped them off too. Yvonna squinted in pain because the thongs had rubbed her raw.

"Don't hurt me," she begged looking back at him. "I'll do anything you say just please don't hurt me."

"Didn't I tell you not to say shit?" He asked as he pressed up against her back to reach her ear. He placed more force on her than necessary.

She nodded yes.

"Then why da fuck you speakin'?" Sprinkles of spit touched her face.

She didn't respond.

"Don't say shit else!" He continued as he busied himself with the pussy he was about to take.

As he captured her silence, he entered her raw. His dick

had grown a solid seven inches. He was so hard that if he'd been any harder, it would've felt like a bat going in and out of her tiny body. The veins on his dick were pulsating as he fucked her without remorse for how she felt. Licking his lips, he caught a brief glimpse of his balls slapping against her phat ass. When he realized he was being turned on even more, and on the verge of cumming before he wanted to, he allowed her ass cheeks to drop against his stomach. With one hand pressing on the small of her back to keep the arch, he grabbed her hair and used it as a reign to ride her from behind.

"Shit!! I'm bout to cum!" He moaned. He had her in the perfect position and could no longer hold out.

Hearing this, Yvonna decided there was no way she was about to be left hanging. She slyly backed up into him and twirled her hips with each motion he made.

CARTEL PUBLICATIONS TITLES

Cartel Publications Order Form
www.thecartelpublications.com
Inmates ONLY get novels for $10.00 per book!

tles		Fee
yt List	_____	$15.00
yt List 2	_____	$15.00
bulls In A Skirt	_____	$15.00
bulls In A Skirt 2	_____	$15.00
ctoria's Secret	_____	$15.00
ison	_____	$15.00
ison 2	_____	$15.00
ll Razor Honeys	_____	$15.00
ll Razor Honeys 2	_____	$15.00
Hustler's Son 2	_____	$15.00
ack And Ugly As Ever	_____	$15.00
ar of The Crack Mom		$15.00
e Face That Launched		
Thousand Bullets	_____	$15.00
e Unusual Suspects	_____	$15.00
ss Wayne & The		
eens of DC	_____	$15.00

ease add $2.00 per book for shipping and handling.

e Cartel Publications * P.O. Box 486 * Owings Mills * MD * 21117

me: _____

dress: _____

y/State: _____

ntact # & Email:
_____

Please allow 5-7 business days for delivery. The Cartel is not responsible for prison orders rejected.

I've never felt more sexier than the way I do now. Strength comes with focusing on your dreams defying all those who stand in your way. I adore the love affair I have with my readers. And I owe the NEW swag in my hips to you.

T. Styles
President &
CEO,
The Cartel
Publications

MEAN GIRLS MAGAZINE

In 2009, we will blast into the industry with the same force Lil' Kim brought with her first album, HARDCORE. This new magazine will tackle real issues from sex to entrepreneurship. But unlike other magazines, we'll do it with some swag. The audience who appreciates hot street literature will enjoy how our story lines are delivered. There isn't a magazine on the market that will hit as hard as we will.

- -

VISIT WWW.MEANGIRLSMAGAZINE.COM FOR SUBSCRIPTION INFORMATION

NAME: _____
ADDRESS: _____
EMAIL: _____

CPSIA information can be obtained
at www.ICGtesting.com
Printed in the USA
LVHW040048251121
704426LV00006B/777

9 780979 493126

and that's why she's drawing a blank."

"She recalled everything up to Bonnydoon. It's not amnesia. She phoned New York from the station. She got a bit confused, she called her ex-boyfriend. Then she sorted it out. She called her boss at Beverley Auctions, she's their wine expert, that's big bucks. Her boss told her to stay at The Four Seasons on the company tab. What am I missing?"

"Her childhood in Sweden, her early experience with sex watching Ingmar Bergman films, no, I think you've covered it all."

"Until the disconnect, between hearing the ring-man executed in the wine shed and turning up on your doorstep with his hand in her purse."

"And a gun."

"A smoking gun."

"So, there's got to be a major traumatic experience in there, you figure, more than being abducted across an international boundary and bearing witness to murder?"

"Yeah, that's what I think," said Morgan.

"And she ends up at The Four Seasons on an expense account. Tomorrow she'll shop."

"Envious? Yeah, but Spivak told her not to leave town, not without us, so she's gotta have supplies."

"From Yorkville, Hazelton Lanes, already."

"So she's trapped in the most fashionable part of the city. She hasn't much choice."

"Trapped? The thing about The Four Seasons, Morgan —"

"It's very expensive."

"Elegant."

"In an expensive sort of way."

"What else is there?"

"You ever stay there?"

"With Philip? No. We had dinner. Met for lunch once. But for ... private times ... we came back here."

"Always?"

"Yeah. Don't look so shocked."

"I'm not shocked. Disappointed, maybe."

"Jealous."

"No, I'm a grown-up. Disappointed *for* you that it couldn't have been better."

"Is that genuine sympathy, Morgan? Or condescension?"

"Yes," he said, with careful equivocation.

There was a long pause. They were friends. Neither felt rancour for breaching bounds of propriety. As partners used to being together in soul-draining crises, their rules of intimacy were elastic. There was no urgency, as there might be between lovers, to resolve the differences between them.

"Morgan, know what I think?" Miranda eventually said.

"What?"

"I think you should knock that back and go home."

"Yeah."

"We're meeting her for breakfast. Maybe she'll put it on her tab. We need a treat."

"Okay," he said, getting up from the old rocker and, after a futile flick of the light switch, walking down the dark hall. "See you tomorrow. Nine o'clock."

"Too early. She won't be up."

"Nine thirty."

He stepped out into the illuminated gloom of the corridor, drawing her door shut behind him.

brick and cantilevered exterior stairs of cement slab and wood. The overall effect was absolute hybrid, what he described as Victorian postmodern, and curiously pleasing.

He had bought it after he and his wife separated, before the divorce.

He stood at the door, his hand on the latch, staring into its gleaming midnight-blue depths.

Lucy was on his mind. That had been years ago, when he was still in his twenties. Twenty-four. She had come here, once, just after he moved in. He was painting the door, the last of a dozen coats, trying for the patina of depth that layers of paint can give wood, like the doors of Dublin. She tried to seduce him. It was her idea of how to negotiate a reconciliation.

He had married the wrong woman. His marriage to Lucy could be measured in months.

The condo was a white elephant, which from Morgan's point of view was a good thing. The architect-builders were happy to arrange for a private mortgage with a minuscule down payment, on the promise of his salary with the police force. The Cabbagetown of his childhood was a world away, just down a few blocks, the other side of Yonge Street.

Miranda had trouble getting to sleep. The mattress was new. The morning he spent cleaning up, Morgan had arranged to have the old one hauled away and this one delivered. She had already slept on the new mattress once, but in a deep, dreamless slumber. She knew she must have been dreaming, but she had not remembered anything on awakening except a sort of bleak vacuum enticing her back into sleep.

That was the previous night. Now she was sure she could feel the trough in the centre of the bed, as if Philip were lying there, still, drawing her to him.

She missed Philip in a strange way. The unknowable qualities about him were part of his attraction. It had never occurred to her the mystique was anything more than a protective vestment to keep his daughters in Oakville from harm, to avoid hurting his wife, to protect Miranda.

Their last hours together remained a blur, even though she had reconstructed an account of everything leading up to the Dom Pérignon. She tried to remember their first meeting. In the courthouse corridor. She was coming out of the washroom. He was rushing headlong down the corridor. They collided.

She could see it all in her mind's eye, not cinematically but in a busy mosaic of images and sounds, a flurry of words and conflicting emotions.

"Damnit, you moron," she had said, while simultaneously trying to ascertain if it was a judge, deserving an instant apology.

"I'm so sorry," he said, helping her to maintain balance. "Did I hurt you? I was clumsy."

"No," she snapped, but looking at his sheepish smile she continued. "Possibly, yes — are you a lawyer?"

"Yes, I am. I was distracted. Are you really?"

"Hurt?"

"Yes."

"No."

"My name is Philip Carter."

Miranda realized, as it all came back, how playful it had been, their initial conversation. Then why was he rushing? Where was he going in such a hurry that he could switch so abruptly to a debonair mode. He didn't explain and it never occurred to her to ask. They went out for dinner that night. She talked mostly about the case she had been attending.

He had seemed surprised she was a detective. Perhaps too surprised. People in that building were usually officers of the court, one way or another, or they were at the court's mercy.

When she explained she was a witness for the defense, he seemed amused.

"Hostile, I assume?"

"No, not really." It registered in the back of her mind that he was using terms more familiar to American courtroom dramas. She wondered how far she should go with this. "You're not working for the prosecution, are you?"

"Me! Do I look like it?" No, he did not. His suit was far too expensive.

"I'm a friendly witness," she said, smiling. "I don't like being this guy's friend, but that's how things worked out."

"This guy, he's a bad guy then."

"Vittorio Ciccone." She enunciated, stressing the consonants as if it were an English name.

He repeated it with an Italian inflection. "He is a bad guy," he added, "a very bad guy. A capital case."

"Murder, yes, first degree."

"And you work Homicide?"

"Yes. And I know, it's strange, but I've been called by the defense. What are you working on?"

"Nothing so interesting. Do you know Ciccone?"

"We've met several times."

"Really. They don't get much bigger than him. What makes you think he's innocent?"

"Not guilty! There's a big difference. Nobody would accuse Vittorio Ciccone of innocence, not even Vittorio Ciccone."

"Should you be talking about this?"

"No, I should not," she said, reassured by his sense of legal propriety.

"Okay," he said. "Tell me about Miranda Quin?"

They sipped their liqueurs, hers a Drambuie and his something more exotic, she didn't catch what. She did not want to talk about herself. She did not want to talk about him, in case he was married.

After a comfortable silence, she said, "He really is one of the bad guys, he's going down for murder...."

"Unless you convince the jury otherwise."

"Yeah, well, that's up to his lawyers. But yes, I could make the difference."

"And then he walks?"

"He walks. For the time being. Sooner or later we'll get him."

"'We? You've switched from 'they' to 'we.'"

"Lawyers are 'they.' 'We' are police."

"And never the twain shall meet — except in this case, you and I, we met in spite of ourselves."

"We did, didn't we," she observed. "It happens. My superintendent is married to a lawyer."

"Rufalo?"

"Yeah, Alex Rufalo. You know him?"

"By reputation. Is he a good man?"

"Yeah, he leaves us alone."

"Us?"

"Me and my partner...."

"Who is?"

"David Morgan." She was surprised he had not heard of Morgan, or that he had not heard of Morgan and herself as a team. They tried to keep out of the papers, but they were well known in the department, big as it was, and among lawyers and judges. That's why she was a valuable asset for the Ciccone defense.

"You're not criminal?" she asked with an disingenuous smile.

"No," he responded with a sly grin. "Corporate. Mostly a desk jockey. Ogilthorpe et al on King Street.

"Gotcha," she said. "That explains the Armani."

"Hugo Boss," he said.

"Gotcha," she said again, only a little disappointed.

As they walked home, choosing Church Street over Yonge to avoid the confusion, where everyone at this time of night seemed dressed for a private masquerade, they did not have much to talk about; they did not yet have a history.

"I've read about Vittorio Ciccone," he ventured.

"Yeah. Drugs. Big time. No record. My partner and I, a couple of years ago, arrested one of his associates for murder. We couldn't connect Ciccone to the crime, not directly, but it was a hit. He arranged it, and the killer, well, honour among thieves, he's doing hard time and Ciccone wasn't charged."

"Then what were you doing in the witness box?"

"You could say I'm a character witness."

"Are you serious?"

"Semi." She caught the look in his eyes as a car drove by. He seemed genuinely interested.

"He lives in Rosedale," she said and prepared to launch into a safe narrative that would incriminate no one, nor

compromise herself. Much as she warmed to this somewhat inscrutable man, she was wary of entrapment. She
did not entirely trust anyone associated with the courts,
especially lawyers, even corporate lawyers.

"A couple of years ago," she continued, "a kid was
killed on his street. A neighbour's little girl. She was
apparently kidnapped. We hoped she was being held for
ransom. We found her body in the ravine. She'd been
brutally assaulted."

"Sexually?"

"And beaten. Some of the bruises were old. My partner
and I, it was our case. We suspected the stepfather but we
couldn't get near him, nothing would stick. Then one day
the stepfather walked into Headquarters and gave himself up. Full confession. His name was Ferguson. It was
Vittorio Ciccone, he got through to the guy. Didn't torture
him, didn't blackmail him, didn't express the community
sentiments by exterminating him. Simply knocked on his
door in Rosedale, told him it was time to turn himself in.
Vittorio Ciccone has that kind of power —"

"Arouses that kind of fear."

"Yeah, but he didn't touch the man, didn't lay a finger
on him."

"And you're going to tell that in court, and the
defense thinks that will get him off for murder?"

"No. It will establish my credentials in relation to
their client."

"And then what?"

"Then," she said, "at the appropriate time, I will say
that I saw him the night of the murder."

"Where?"

"At home. His place, not mine."

Philip Carter looked at her cryptically. She could not tell what he was thinking.

"Last fall," she continued. "I was out for a walk. Rosedale is a beautiful place for long walks alone through autumn leaves on red brick sidewalks, especially in the evening. He was pulling into his drive and caught me in the headlights. He recognized me from the little girl's murder."

"Was he in court for that?"

"No, but we talked during the investigation. And we'd talked before, about the murder his 'associate' went down for. So he saw me, came back out of his garage and we chatted on the street. He invited me in for a drink. He assured me his wife was home. We both laughed. There was no way I was going into Vittorio Ciccone's house for a drink. That was about it."

"That was it? You talked. That makes him innocent."

"It does when the man who was murdered was murdered in Hamilton, same time, an hour's drive away."

"But there were witnesses — weren't there?"

"There was confusion. It was outside a Tim Hortons. A couple of cops stopping in for a donut saw it happen through the window. In spite of the night glare. They said Ciccone got out of his car, walked over to this drug dealer, shot him in the head, a single shot, and drove off. They swear it was Ciccone."

"Did they get his licence?"

"So they say. They rushed out, got his licence, but didn't chase him. They stayed with the dead man, watched him die. They didn't recall the licence number until later that night."

"Ciccone isn't a guy you'd mistake for someone else."

"Exactly, not unless you wanted to."

"You think it's a set-up?"

Miranda stopped. They were under a streetlight, his eyes cast in deep shadow, only pinpricks of light glistening from his pupils. She could not bring his face into focus. She thought how desperately the police wanted to bring the man down. Her new friend's interest puzzled her. She shrugged.

"I couldn't say, I wouldn't say that. I only know that I saw him, and his car, in Rosedale, the same time as the shooting."

"Then —"

"It's not my call."

She was abrupt. Philip let the matter drop and walked her the rest of the way home in congenial silence, leaving her at the security door without making overtures to come in.

The next day they met for lunch. Three days later, they had lunch again and spent the afternoon in bed at her place.

The lobby of The Four Seasons was more self-consciously opulent than either Morgan or Miranda were comfortable with. They came in through separate doors at the same time and converged in the main concourse. Miranda felt an uneasy familiarity. Both of them tried not to look like locals hoping to catch a glimpse of Bruce Willis or maybe a Baldwin.

"Did you call her?" Morgan asked, gazing past Miranda with what he assumed was worldly disinterest.

"No, I thought you would."